THE WILD

matt whyman

Hodder
Children's
Books

A division of Hodder Headline Limited

ISBN 0 340 88453 3

Typeset in Baskerville by Avon DataSet Ltd,
Bidford-on-Avon, Warwickshire

Printed and bound in Great Britain by
Bookmarque Ltd, Croydon, Surrey

The paper and board used in this paperback by Hodder
Children's Books are natural recyclable products made from
wood grown in sustainable forests. The manufacturing
processes conform to the environmental regulations of the
country of origin.

Hodder Children's Books
a division of Hodder Headline Ltd
338 Euston Road
London NW1 3BH

KEY

----- Railway

—·—·— River

——— Border

▨ Sea / Lake

OB'

IRTYSH

Omsk

Petropavlovak

Oostanay
(Kostanay)

Astana ★

ERTIS

ALTAI MTS.

KAZAKHSTAN

rals'k

Baikonur (cosmodrome)

Kareshalan

Lake Balknash

Taraz

Almaty

UZBEKISTAN

KYRGYZSTAN

KMENISTAN

CHINA

Acknowledgement

I should like to thank the following for their help, encouragement and guidance: my editor Emily Thomas, the designer David McDougall, and the entire team at Hodder Children's Books; David Godwin, Sarah Savitt and all at DGA; Ekaterina Girshina; Melvin Burgess; Oksana Romina; Suzanne Joinson; Marina Beylina; Simon Reeve; Kate Joyce; Alla Vasilieva; Nicholas Blincoe; Duncan Perrin; Mary Byrne; Emma and the girls, also Mungo and Butch – the wildest of them all.

Kareshalan Bay, Aral Sea Region, Kazakhstan. This evening:

'Here she comes!'

All eyes turn to the boy with the binoculars, then to the sky he's been scanning so carefully. They've done this before, many times over, but Misha is always the one who sees things ahead of anyone else. The salt wind that sails in across the tundra barely makes him blink, and he's never been tempted to join the others in throwing stones to pass the time. Huge trawlers, schooners and tugboats lie rusting in the sand all around this harbour, good for nothing any more but target practice. Some forty years earlier, an ocean could be found here – a vast inland sea that just dried up when the Soviets laid claim to the river flows to feed their cotton fields. Now, only light ebbs and flows across this man-made disaster zone. Ghost waters, some call it, but with a catch that fell from the heavens.

'Fire up the engine, Alexi!' At once the boy is abandoned as a dozen kids scramble onto the back of a flatbed lorry. Inside the cab, from the bench seat behind the wheel, Misha's older brother twists the ignition key. Black smoke coughs from the exhaust, which shakes until the engine catches.

Alexi Titov has been driving this breathless old beast nearly half his life. Started at nine, the same age as Misha now. Most probably the truck is older than the combined age of every single member of this rag-tag bunch Alexi has recruited, but it can still speed across the former seabed so long as he finds the right gear.

'Jump in, Mish!' Alexi has to repeat himself before the boy comes alive. By God, the little grunt seemed to inhabit another world at times, though everyone valued his sixth sense when it came to spotting space waste.

All of them had seen the rocket go up, way out to the east. This far from the cosmodrome, however, only the vapour trail was really visible: a chalk-white column that had climbed so high the sky seemed more like a vast vertical backdrop than any kind of ceiling. The way the rocket slowly pitched, yawed and rolled would always leave some of the boys unsteady on their feet. If they followed it for long enough, the muscles in their necks would begin to throb and ache. Some even found that it was more comfortable to keep watching by turning around, such was the way these things seemed to arc so deceptively. Even focusing on the glow from the afterburners was no good. That was like staring at a cigarette ember. It would go out eventually, but then you'd only have to close your eyes and there it was again. One by one they would admit their imagination had got the better of them, and look for stones to throw instead.

Only Misha continued to watch beyond the vanishing point, as the vapour thickened, buckled and then faded away. After that, it was just a question of leaving the boy to keep watching the sky. Nobody knew what happened to the rocket once it breached the earth's atmosphere. Most launches were commercial nowadays, intended to deliver satellites into low orbit. What

*interested this gang were the treasures these things jettisoned on
the struggle into space. That's why they have gathered here at
the dusk end of this day, hoping that Alexi's little brother would
set eyes on something beyond them all.*

*Right now, as far as the crew can see, the sky behind the
fishing harbour seems quite at peace. Stars are beginning to
prick the twilight and look set to come out in force. Alexi's
brother rides up front beside him on the bench: milky-pale and
soulful-eyed, but with a shock of black hair like he's just been
stunned by a live wire.*

'Head north,' says Misha. 'She's on her way, I promise.'

*Alexi swings the truck out of the harbour in a spray of sand,
and then punches the accelerator. Beyond the reach of the sea
walls, the ground still shelves where the tide once turned. Now,
there's nothing out there but a desert of scree and scrub.*

*'Are you quite sure?' Alexi grips the wheel with both hands
as the vehicle begins to rattle and shudder. It's never an easy
ride, which is why it has to be worth his while.*

'Wait and see.'

*Another cry directs Alexi's attention to the big wing-mirror.
It's already positioned to show up the sky behind. What he sees
is a spark of light, skipping across the upper reaches like a stone
across water. Then, with a bang, the fireball emerges. At first it
appears to be coming straight at them, but the crew know better
than to duck or run for cover. Instead, all heads turn as a mile-
high trail of flames overtakes the truck and rushes to meet the
horizon. The impact with the ground occurs far up-range. It's
bright as a match head flaring, and just as fleeting too. The
dull boom that follows can barely be heard over the claps and
cheers and whistling.*

3

'Booster rocket!' says Misha. 'Second stage is my guess.'

'How much will that earn us then, genius?' Alexi coaxes another degree from the speedometer, anxious now to claim the prize – whatever it turns out to be.

The two boys bounce and slide about on the bench, but the discomfort is nothing if it means they are first on the scene. If his brother is correct, the titanium panelling and the motor parts will fetch precious dollars from the right people. Providing the cutting equipment doesn't die on them, he and his wrecking crew could have it broken up and lashed onto the back of the truck within hours. Alexi knows full well that the price for it will depend on the mood of their middleman, but he presses his kid brother all the same. 'What do you say? Is this our ticket out of here?'

Just then, the nearside tyres crash in and out of a rut in the seabed. The vehicle jumps violently, which prompts curses from the crew out back. Only the boy riding shotgun says nothing. Wrestling the truck under his control again, Alexi instructs them to hang in there and prays they won't suffer a blowout. It's a hazard of such hostile terrain, but then lives have come to depend on a run such as this. He chances another glance at his brother, as concerned for him as he is for their safe passage over the sands. There sits little Mish with those scuffed binoculars in his lap and his sight fused to the horizon. His eyes are narrowed, but gleam in this last light like the detonation the boys have just witnessed. Alexi tightens his grip on the wheel, squeezing that gas pedal now. The sooner they reach the crash site, he thinks, the quicker they can take off themselves.

1

You need faith to believe a sea was once here. In our lives, that is something constantly put to the test. I have heard the trawlermen's stories and seen photographs of great catches handed down two generations now. Sometimes, it really can seem too good to be true. These tales contain such life and joy, while the colour in the pictures is vibrant and unreal.

When you look up from these old snapshots, it's hard not to think perhaps this region is what has faded over time. From the seasons to the faces, the soil and the sky, everything seems so washed out.

The stagnant puddle out to the west somewhere is all that remains. It's little more than a joke, really. Shells in among the feather grass should be proof to those kids who think the boats were hauled here to fool us. But then how in God's name can a tide go out and never come back again? Most of us try not to dwell on it like a lot of old folk. Nor do we shake our fists at the north and blame Mother Russia – that's what the truly embittered call the country they hold responsible. The way I see things, it's all history. The ruling party that decided to play around with the rivers are dead and buried now.

Had they left the water flows alone, we might still be netting sturgeon and harvesting orchards around the coast, but that's just how it is. We are the children of Aral, not her relics. Indeed the only mother in our lives today is nature. She may be cruel, but she has raised us to be tough.

Even if I were from the generation that still rages at Russia, my loyalties would be torn. Thanks to our grandfather, my brother and I have a drop of the old superpower in our blood. He came to Kazakhstan from Siberia, a remote and unforgiving Russian region, and we have inherited his wolf-brown eyes and fierce sense of survival. In his time, he went to great lengths to reason that what had happened to us here was not down to spite or malice. Nobody would purposely destroy a sea so that everything around it perished. It was simply a mistake in a Soviet programme to cultivate crops that has since become history, just like the sea itself.

Whatever the reasons for the disappearance of the ocean, those who claim they grew up on her shores believe one day they will see water here again. Who will pull off such a miracle, and how, I do not know. Oil is what seems to interest outsiders, but all we see of it are the drilling rigs and the pipelines that carry it out of here. Word is that scientists have been seeding trees in a bid to breathe another kind of life into the region. Like my friends, I've learned not to place much hope in any kind of transformation. Holding out for a fresh start just leads to the same kind of feelings that affect those who remember the sea. It can eat away at your lust for life if all you do is sit on a porch, play dominoes and wait.

Instead, we make the most of what we have, and let nobody stand in our way. The rewards on offer may not amount to much, but we throw ourselves into each opportunity with all our heart and spirit. What choice do we have?

'Go easy on the gas, Alexi! You're too young to die, and I'm just too damn pretty!'

This is Denis. I only just hear him over the complaint of the engine, but I can be sure that he speaks for everyone in the back of the truck. Most of my younger hired-hands had run to join us from the playground beside our apartment block. Even so, there are one or two crew members on board who come with me every time we leave the harbour, and Denis is top of the list. He is seventeen, one year older than me, but he frets for us all like we're his babies. If I slow to a speed that satisfies Denis, we might as well get out and walk. One time, he moaned so much about my driving that I made him take the wheel to see if he could do a better job. He stalled her twice over twenty metres, and then refused to go any further because everyone was giving him a tough time. I gave him plenty of respect later that day, once I'd reclaimed my seat and reached our destination so that he could go to work. As well as clapping him on the back for a job well done he received twenty-five United States dollars – his share from the scrap we had gone on to sell.

Denis may be a first-class worrier but he also happens

to be the very best when it comes to carving up space waste and extracting the valuables. Present him with any seared and mangled wreck, he'll open it up like a surgeon and let nothing go to waste. A couple of times we have laid claim to entire satellites. Now that really is like striking gold. Every now and then, the guys at mission control will bring an old one back to earth. Usually we would know about it a day in advance because the jeeps from the *militzia* would be out patrolling the area. With Misha's foresight, we have been known to beat them all to it. Even so, we must work like the devil is closing in on us to get the parts onto the truck. We can't afford to leave anything behind. Even the tyre prints have to be covered up around the crash site, in case a rival crew chooses to track us down.

Right now, I can see Denis in my rear-view mirror, fighting to hold onto the roll bar and keep his nose and mouth covered with his shawl. Like the rest of my crew, he's wearing a pair of ex-army tank goggles. They make him look like a human fly, but if you're riding in the back they're kind of compulsory. We have all grown used to living with sand in our eyes and throats and nostrils. It is the pesticide that can make it unbearable – a parting gift from our poisoned ocean. Running off the cotton fields and into the rivers, these chemicals had killed just the fish at first. Then the waters dried up and it settled into the sand. The stuff is here to stay now, cooked in with the salt left behind by the sea. It looks like snow out of season, and just drifts and spreads everywhere. What was once farmland around the coastline looks no different than

8

the seabed nowadays, all because of this toxic cocktail. It leaves a bad taste in everyone's mouth, and can bring on tears that sting and are hard to stop.

'Denis,' I shout over the din, and grin into the rear-view mirror, 'do us a favour, huh? Cover your whole face for me. It's upsetting to see you there every time I check behind.'

'Then keep your eyes up front, goddamn it! Concentrate on not killing us!'

'We're all going to die some day,' I remind him, and lift both hands from the wheel. In the mirror, I see the expression change on his face. 'Why don't we all go together?'

'Don't be a madman,' he protests as the truck begins to veer. 'We want to get there in one piece!'

I grab the wheel again, only to kick back a gear so the engine screams and lurches. In the rear-view, I see Denis wheel his arms helplessly in a bid to balance. Cackling now, I squeeze the accelerator and watch my friend tip onto the floor of the truck.

'We want to get there *first*!' I yell at him, and I mean every word. For I doubt we are the only crew to spot this tumbling treasure. Salvagers like us are constantly roaming the seabed and the scrub surrounding it. We are like jackals, so the space agency likes to describe us. They claim the rocket parts that drop to earth remain state property, but out here it belongs to whoever gets there first. Should we be lucky enough to fall upon the scorched metal corpse in question, we'll rip it up and break it down, just like the pack of animals they believe us to be. For this isn't just a wasteland to us. This is a *hunting* ground.

'Buckle up,' I tell my brother, locking my own belt into place. 'I need to know you're safe.'

2

Winter is on the way. All of us sense it coming. I like this time of year best of all. Our summers can be suffocating, while the frosts we expect very soon are just as unforgiving. The wind never gives up, whatever the season, but this evening it's not too hot or cold. Some of my crew are stripped down to their vests, in fact. They wear nickel dog tags round their necks, just for decoration, as well as old boots we like to think once belonged to soldiers killed in action.

Military gear is easy to pick up from the former fish markets, and that includes the pistol packed under my seat. It's there for reassurance, along with the torch, jack and toolbox. We even have a radio in this truck, but there's rarely anything on it from one end of the dial to the other. If we travel far we can sometimes make out faint voices and religious music, but mostly it's just empty noise. Misha would happily keep it on in case we passed within range of a transmission of some sort. I just don't like it. The static reminds me of Geiger counters – those magic wands that scientists sometimes bring out here to test for radiation. It was the Soviets who once used the steppes as a testing ground for atomic bombs. We are

11

told there is nothing to fear, so many miles down south, but then the winds don't answer to officials. Denis says I really ought to make room under the bench here for a cheap counter at the very least. I just refuse to live in fear.

Within half an hour of setting off, we've put thirty miles on the clock. I have made this crossing many times, a shortcut across the seabed to the drop zone beyond, but each journey is so different because the drifting sands change everything. Some dunes have built up since I was last here, but then I can't be sure that I've been here at all. The only thing I know is that we're a long way from home, and our headlamps cut through darkness now.

'Are we lost?' I say, partly to myself. 'Tell me we're not lost.'

The old sea floor just seems to rush at us from nowhere: an uneven sprawl of desert, grit and grass, frosted white by salt. At this speed the truck threatens to shake apart. I have to concentrate hard, but at any time it would come as a shock to hear someone tapping on my side window, and then a muffled voice: 'Alexi, I need to speak to you.'

I glance round with a start and see the face of a girl with more balls than most. It's Lena, my hired gun, up close against the glass. She's standing on the footplate with a casual grip on my wing-mirror and the roll bar. Her thick, dark hair flies sideways across her face, but it doesn't hide her idiot grin.

'What are you doing?' I push open the quarter light, half laughing at her stupidity. The wind whistles through

12

the gap, but she can hear me now. 'Get back before you're thrown off!'

'Just stretching my legs,' she grins.

I try to see if she's being serious behind her goggles, though I can't afford to be distracted for more than a blink. Lena has never had much respect for her own safety, which is perhaps why she always volunteers to stand guard whenever we set to work. Like many kids in the region, she'd seen so many family members get sick and fade away that she had become almost immune to fear. She could have got my attention just by thumping on the roof of the cab like Denis and everyone else, but not Lena. I've warned her before about climbing all over my truck at speed, but she only listens to me when I hand over my pistol and tell her to watch out for bandits.

'I have a message for you, too,' she tells me next, coming closer to the quarter light so we can hear. 'The boys are saying we should switch on the search lamp. We're driving nearly blind.'

The lamp is mounted on the roof of the cab. We use it to see what we're doing once we've found the crash site. It's also visible from miles around, not just to other scavengers but the recovery squads dispatched by the cosmodrome, which is why we can't afford to switch it on yet.

'The spotter planes could be overhead at any time,' I remind her. 'Now please get back where you belong and let me concentrate on the driving.'

Lena salutes me, still goofing around, and then raps on the glass to address my brother. 'I hope you know where you're going, little man,' she yells across the cab. 'Alexi would be lost without you.'

'Get out of here!' I laugh, shaking my head when she finally sees sense.

I am very fond of Lena, even if she can be a little dangerous at times. We were born in the same month and year, but the similarities end there. She'd sooner pull a trigger on a gun to see if it is loaded, than check the magazine for bullets. It's as if she lives her life with the safety catch off, which earns respect from me and demands not a little caution. I only really got to know her when she quit fighting with boys, and became their protector instead. Sometimes I catch her playing with her hair. If she sees me she will stop and blush a little bit, or just glare at me until I look away.

I hear the rest of the crew cheering now as they haul her onto the back of the truck once more, and wonder what my brother must make of it all. I chance a look across at him, there on the bench just like me. What sets him apart is the fact that his stare appears to have turned inwards. I look at him again, alarmed by what this could mean.

'Misha, are you with us?' My efforts have been focused on getting across this terrain without tipping over or tearing off an axle. All of a sudden I wonder if my muttering about gaining ground has fallen on deaf ears. It just feels like he isn't here. Knowing what I do about my brother's state of health, that's enough to alarm me. Each jolt from this journey seems to pass through him unnoticed. Everyone else continues to swear and joke about the hiding they have planned for me unless I go easy, but only one thing concerns me now. This would not be a good time for Mish to have one of his 'moments', which is all we can bear to call them. We're travelling way too fast for me to check him out properly, but if I have to stop then so be it. Even if it means losing out on our haul. 'Mish?' I call again, and resort to punching his shoulder. '*Speak to me*!' I switch my foot from the accelerator to the brake, only to stamp hard on the gas once more when Misha responds with a punch of his own.

'Keep going, Alexi, I'm fine! Will you please stop being so twitchy and let me work out where we're going.'

He settles back on the bench, and so do I, but with a big sigh of relief. I feel stupid, and yet quietly pleased that it was all in my head and not his. Mish may have simply tuned out just then, but I know sometimes that marks the calm before a storm.

'So do you want to give me directions?' I ask, my sense of relief doing little to ease the pressure I'm under to keep driving like a demon.

'You can steer a little more to the east, but I don't think we'll miss this one.'

I do as I'm told, then hit the wipers to clear the dust. It's a clear night, and I'm willing to believe that my brother can use the stars as a map. I certainly don't know my way around the heavens, and would be lost without him. All I can do is take care of what's happening around us, even if the darkness at this level makes it hard to be sure where the dunes meet the sky.

'How much further?' I ask, now that I'm sure I have his attention. 'Don't just say "ten minutes". You always say that to shut me up, and I don't believe you any more.'

'Less than ten,' he chuckles, and turns his attention to me for the first time since we set off. I shoot him a look that says he'd better not be bullshitting, and then he invites me to see for myself. I glance out of my side window, find nothing to report, and that's when the seabed in my headlights just seems to rise up like a wave.

'Hold on!' I yell, as I realise what's happening. 'This is going to be big.' I hadn't seen the old shoreline coming, a bar of sand I can't avoid, and the engine races as we travel over the crest. Immediately, I think we're going to twist too far, only for the truck to crash back down on one rear wheel and then the rest – a perfect landing, I would boast at any other time. As it is, I slide to a dead halt and just stare through the windscreen without blinking. Denis breaks the silence by erupting in the back. He clambers to his feet and pounds the lid of the cabin, only to be struck dumb like the others by what my brother had foreseen.

'Mother of God,' I hear him whistle.

I look at little Misha again, his face lit up like mine, but mostly from the patches of grass still burning ahead of the crash site. For we've stopped at the foot of a long, scorched carpet of scrub, and at the far end lies our booster rocket: second stage, just as my brother had said, and as big as a stranded ship. The way it's shaped we could be looking at a goblet dropped by the gods – or 'a trophy', I hear someone say. Denis snaps on the search lamp now, and this colossal hunk of smouldering space junk lights up like a diamond on display.

'Just look at her,' I declare. 'She is a *beauty*!'

3

It's been just over six months since Misha's first seizure. At the time we all thought he was fooling around. One minute he had been chattering away about spotting the difference between a star and a satellite flaring at sunset, the next his eyes went wide and he just seemed to shut down. Looking back, it was as if a spirit voice had suddenly commanded him to be quite still. Then he began to shiver inexplicably, as if that current we'd always joked about really was flowing through him. I still feel bad about laughing along with everyone else, even when he crumpled to the floor. It was only when we noticed he had urinated in his shorts that we realised this was no joke.

Since then, my brother has suffered many more moments. We call them that to make it seem like something he'll always get through. A seizure just sounds so final, as if perhaps he might stop working permanently. I am always on guard for the next one, and like to keep a constant eye on him. If Misha falls quiet, as if lost to us all, I am the first to snap my fingers in front of his face and then create a safe space if it's clear that he isn't coming back without a fight. There is little I can do when it happens but make sure he doesn't fall awkwardly, swallow his tongue, or vomit and choke. A moment can last a matter of seconds or sometimes a couple of minutes. To me, it always goes on for a lifetime. There have been times when all I want to do is hug my little brother so tight that his body can't shake and twitch and writhe, but I have been advised that restraint could harm him. Often I wish someone could watch over me, but it would mean bringing the truth home to our poor father about the condition of his second son. For it isn't just something little Mish will grow out of, as I have led him to believe. It's a tumour on his brain, taking shape like a shadow at sunset – before everything turns to black.

For too many people in this region, death comes early. According to the doctors, it is no wonder – when everything we touch, eat and breathe is so contaminated. We don't have enough medicines or equipment, either, which is why the treatment for a serious illness is often the same.

'Pack your bags and leave.' That's what the nurse from the sanatorium had advised me, when I first carried Mish there for help. She lived in the same apartment block as us, the one behind the disused canning factory, and knew that I looked after my little brother. I tried to tell her more about what had just happened to him, but she stopped me when the knot in my throat became too big to budge. 'Take him to a city. Any place but here.'

The sanatorium stands at the far end of the north beach, which is the best place to see dust storms billowing in. It's a single-storey concrete block, built several decades ago when most people accepted that the sea wasn't coming back. Tuberculosis was the big threat at the time. Then, over the years, the place became worn out from dealing with many more conditions and complaints. Every month or so, a small team of medics would show up from the relief agency, but that's when *everyone* seemed to get sick. Mostly it was down to the staff to do what they could with what little they had, even if it went beyond the call of duty.

'What about tests?' I had asked the nurse when she made her diagnosis. She had arranged a bed so Misha could rest and then invited me outside to talk – off the record, so she kept saying, as if her job depended on it. 'You can't be sure it's a tumour without tests,' I continued, my voice sounding close to cracking. I was shocked that she could just say such a thing by simply looking at my brother, just as I was by what it might mean.

'You're right,' she said. 'But we just don't have the resources, and you can't afford to wait around. What I can offer you is experience. I have seen too many people show up here with lesser symptoms and never get better again.'

'Maybe it was a one-off,' I had countered, searching for a reason. 'Perhaps something just misfired in his brain. My truck sometimes cuts out for no reason. All I have to do is clean the plugs and everything is fine again.'

'Even if you brought him in complaining of a headache,' she replied, 'I'd give you the same advice. Alexi Titov, I pray that I am wrong, but the longer you stay then all we can do is assume the worst. I could admit him, but what good would that do? This environment is what has made him sick. Aral is the infection. It's a hot zone, and no hospital or clinic here is immune. Specialists exist who can help your brother, but you need to travel to them . . .' The nurse had paused there, considering me for a moment. 'Have you been to the old capital before?' she asked. 'Could you afford to go that far?'

Almaty, once our capital city, lies five hundred miles to the southeast, near the border with China. I told her I had never set foot outside the Aral region, but that I would take a train to the ends of the earth if it meant saving my kid brother. She seemed relieved, found a little pad and pencil in her coat pocket and started writing. She told me it was the name and address of a charity hospital where kids like us were welcomed. Almaty sported the best medical and educational facilities our country could offer. I didn't care why the government had decided to move out of the city and start over in the north of the country. I had just heard that it still offered more than any other place in Kazakhstan, even if that didn't amount to much.

'Do you remember Anatoli Zenkov?' she asked. 'The little boy from the apartment on the ground floor of our block – the one that faced the swings.'

'With the dog called Rebel?' I said, to check. 'Yes, I remember that boy. He had milky discs in his eyes.'

'Those were cataracts,' she said. 'His mother took him to Almaty for an operation last month. I hear from a colleague out there that he can see clearly again now.'

'So he didn't come home again?'

She looked surprised at what I had said, unsure why anyone would consider this place as somewhere you would want to be.

'That was their choice, Alexi. Just as your brother deserves the same thing: a choice.'

'But what do I tell him?'

I felt numb from what had happened, but deep inside I knew I couldn't afford to stay that way for long. If I was going to save Misha, I would need money – and fast.

'Tell your brother that you'll do whatever you can for him,' she said eventually, nodding to herself as if this was all she could offer. 'Wherever it may take you, let him know he's not alone.'

I didn't follow her back into the sanatorium straight away. I stayed on the beach for a few minutes instead, facing into the wind so my cheeks would dry faster. I wanted to be sure that when I saw Misha I would be strong for him – and I haven't let him down yet.

That nurse had no right to make any kind of diagnosis, but I knew she had his best interest at heart. The sanatorium is the only health care we have here. It's really just a bunch of beds with broken-down ventilators in a back room. Our mother passed away here five years before. A slow death by sadness, it seemed to her young sons at the time. All I know is she had refused to leave this land that would basically kill her. She just wasn't prepared to be apart from her family. But when she went for ever she seemed to take our father in spirit.

Yasha Titov rarely ventures out of our apartment

nowadays, choosing instead to sit at the window with his memories. Like my grandfather, Papa had worked as a stevedore, unloading trawlers at the dockside when they came in with their catches. One time, a crane dropped a palette loaded with fish as Papa had been directing it out of a hold. The accident crushed the bones in one of his feet so badly that he lost all feeling in it. His job meant everything to him, however, and for years after that he continued to work at the dockside office – processing bill tickets and marine insurance forms. Then the sea began her slow retreat, and finally he lost his living as well. Like many men in the region, he found it impossible to accept. Our father took to bickering with former colleagues about what had happened. He became someone who could be angered by everything and nothing at all, and so we kept our distance. When our mother passed away, I think he realised what should've been most important to him, and just sort of died with her.

Yasha is a defeated man now, in body and in spirit. When I found out about Misha's condition, I worried about how my father would take it. I believed he would blame the rocket parts we handle, and maybe try to confiscate the keys to the truck. Many people claim the chemicals in the fuel could mess with minds, but I just couldn't afford to stop salvaging – even if it had caused my brother's illness in the first place. The money we made from it was our ticket out of here, which was why I chose to keep the truth from Papa.

Convincing Yasha that the seizures were just a harmless phase turned out to be much easier than I had expected.

I simply told him we had been advised not to worry. Like Mish, he accepted my word without question. I did wonder whether both of them were in some kind of denial, which made me all the more determined not to let them down. Unlike my father, locked away inside his own home, I have done my mourning for one lifetime. I have grown up with loss all around me, and refuse to let go of anything more.

Misha needs my help now, and I will be there for him until he is well again. Whatever it takes, I will do it. I am not scared. I can't afford to be. He is my brother, after all. My flesh, blood and bone.

4

'Alexi!' my brother cries now, and I realise I am alone in the cab with my thoughts. I squint through the windscreen and see him facing me from the blackened strip of scrub. Mish is shielding his eyes from the searchlight, his silhouette laid out behind him. Some of my crew have already reached the booster rocket, which dwarfs them all. It's way too big to be simply dragged from the site by towing cable, and will take longer than I had planned to break down into moveable parts. I hear a thud from the back of the truck. In the wing-mirror, I see Denis jump and wheel around.

'Careful, you clowns!' he yells. 'And put that cigarette out. If the gas tank is leaking we'll all go up in flames!'

Those goggles of his have come off, replaced now by a pair of round, wire-framed glasses. He's barking orders at two identical giants on the tailgate now: twin brothers Anton and Maxim. In response, one of them flicks the tail end of his roll-up into the night, while the other bows his head. They're hired for their strength as well as their silence. Even when Denis gets a little sensitive about the way they handle his cutting equipment, they'll do as they are told. The twins might not think too quickly, but they can work as a unit without exchanging a word, and see a job through to the end.

I switch my attention back to the booster rocket, still stunned by the sheer size of it. Climbing from the cab now, I can't help grinning when I think that brother and I might soon be out of here.

'Comrades,' I crow, hoping to stir them by sounding like an old general, 'let's go to work! I want the ropes and the sledgehammer over there now; also the clamps – if we're going to prise off the plating first. Lena, I need you here.'

Lena had just found a foothold on the rocket's flare pipe when I say this. A couple of the others have already scrambled to the upper rim, looking like monk vultures on a kill. I reach back into the cab, find the pistol under the bench. By the time my hired gunhand has reached me, I've got it locked and loaded.

'That must've been lifting some payload,' she says, jabbing a thumb over her shoulder. 'Another Mars mission, you think?'

I say nothing, leaving Lena to believe what she wants. Frankly, I don't care what it was, so long as the *militzia* aren't out in force looking for it.

'If they ever put a man on the red planet,' she continues, despite my silence, 'he should be from Aral. We're the toughest sons of bitches on this earth, and we lost all our water as well.' Lena kicks at a crust of salt beneath her feet, watches it shower across the sand. She looks up at me again, and then out across the scrub under the stars. 'The way I see things, it would be like home from home.'

'Lena, this place is more savage than Mars. Up there you don't see security choppers springing from the horizon threatening all kinds through loudhailers. That's why I'm relying on you to keep lookout.'

'I know that.' She chews on her lip, considering me for a moment. 'Are you OK, Alexi? It isn't every day we get a rocket this size. You don't seem so thrilled.'

I place the gun in her open palm, watch her fingers close around it.

'I just can't afford to screw up,' I say, and find Misha over her shoulder. He's with the others, helping to carry the equipment and laughing a little too late at a joke that's just been cracked. Everyone knows about his condition, and my vow to get help for him. It just isn't something ever mentioned in front of Mish himself. Maybe they can't find the right words, or perhaps they're reluctant to face up to it. Either way, it's clear they keep some distance from him. This saddens me, because we're all outsiders here. Lena must pick up on my thoughts from the way I watch them. For she slips the pistol into the waistband under her vest, and assures me that our time has come.

'We're going to serve up this chunk of junk to our man for breakfast, my friend. By sunrise you'll have all the money you need so your brother can get better. You'll see.'

'I hope you're right, Lena. We need to be out of here before the winter sets in, so this one has to count.'

Many things went into hibernation when the frosts arrived, including the cosmodrome. Such was the risk of

29

parts seizing up on the launch pad that only test missiles were fired throughout the season, and there was nothing left to salvage from them. For three months every year, my crew split up to fend for themselves. When the ground froze it proved treacherous for the truck, and so it was only natural for everyone to be drawn to whatever means of survival they could find. The younger ones simply went home and begged or stole on behalf of their families. Some of us continued to scavenge for scrap, heading on by foot in search of old Soviet bunkers and underground stores. There were dozens dotted around the region. Most had been plundered over the years and stripped to the sockets. Those that remained untouched were buried under sand. Transformed into tombs trapped in time. Finding them wasn't easy. You had to scour the frozen desert for antenna spikes and razorwire, and then risk frostbite in your fingers as you clawed around for a way in. Sometimes gaining entry proved impossible. Other times it was all too easy, but often for a reason.

Together with the twins, I uncovered only one installation the year before. It had nearly killed us digging down to find the hatch, and with some help from a monkey wrench we turned the flywheel quick enough. As soon as the seal cracked apart, however, an oddly sweet smell like turning fruit forced us all back for a moment. Anton had been the first to go in, just as soon as the stench cleared, only to return with a ghost-white face covered in dust. It wasn't a bunker or even a missile silo, he reported, but a laboratory of some description. Neither of us could stop Maxim from checking out what had spooked his brother so badly. He came back in a similar shape, and said he had seen fridges down there containing racks of phials and test tubes. Many were slapped with biohazard stickers, so he told us, which persuaded us to abandon the site altogether. The fridges would've earned us good money, and God knows we could've cleaned up with the chemicals, but nobody was prepared to go down again. I didn't want to face another winter as hard as that one, and I could sense that Lena felt the same way.

'We'll make this night count,' she agrees, and turns now for the sand bar. 'By the time the sun shows up tomorrow morning, people will know we're the best in the business.'

I watch Lena take her place on the ridge, facing out into the darkness with nothing but her cigarettes for company. Most of my crew have smoked from an early age, and I am no exception. Over the next half an hour, I get through one cigarette after another while throwing out orders and instructions to my crew, as well as spare tobacco. Like everyone else, I figured the air was so polluted we might as well make the most of it. Only Misha has never been tempted, which simply serves to mark him out all the more.

When I catch up with my brother, I find him watching Denis hard at work. A concentrated flame roars from the nozzle of my friend's cutting torch. He's on his knees, with Misha standing right behind him, at work on the belly of our prey. The twins, meanwhile, have just cut loose a ring around the flare pipe, and appeal for help to slip it free. It's just so much bigger than anything we've handled before, and I wonder whether Lena was right. Maybe it had just driven another mission to Mars into space. We had made such a mess of this world, it was only natural that we'd look to start again.

A shower of sparks spits over Denis's shoulder just then and falls at my brother's feet. When Denis becomes aware of him there, he flips up his goggles and glowers angrily. 'Kid, smell the air for me.'

Misha does as he is asked. I cringe at how simple he must seem, even though I know there is so much more going on inside.

'Give him a break,' I ask, but Denis chooses to ignore me.

'Do you know what it is?' he continues. 'Let me tell you. It's rocket propellant. Think of it as supercharged gasolene, and look what I'm holding here.' He shows him the blue flame. 'Now, I get paid a couple bucks more for being suicidal, and you don't, so back off!'

'Easy,' I say, coming between them now. 'Mish just likes to see the expert at work.'

'You could get a crowbar in there now.' My brother gestures at the blackened incision that Denis has made in the rocket housing. 'That panel should break off easily enough, then I can carry it back.'

Denis shoots me a look, and then gestures gruffly for me to pass him the crowbar. It's lying in his toolkit just in front of me, but Misha grabs it for him first. Denis bristles, seems to think about the situation, and then moves to one side.

'Go ahead then, little man. Show us what you can do.'

'Really?' Mish shifts his attention between us, unsure if this is a joke.

'If it means you'll take away the damn panel and leave me in peace.'

'*Yes!*' Without warning, my brother swings the crowbar around and drives it into the gash Denis has created. He gives it a couple of cranks and the panel pops clean away.

'Impressed?' I ask Denis under my breath.

'The kid got lucky,' he says begrudgingly. 'The panel was just hanging by a thread.'

I find him grinning at me, but that leaves his face in a flash when a cry goes up from the sandbank.

It's Lena, raising the alarm: '*Incoming!*'

I spin around, as my crew respond by dropping away from the rocket. I see Lena pull back from the ridge, looking like she is about to turn and scramble for cover. Instead, she reaches round for the pistol, goes back up with it drawn in both hands. And then, like ghost wraiths rising, bright beams of light float into the darkness behind her.

5

A pause falls over the crash site. It lasts just long enough for everyone to take on board what is going on. For now we can hear engines buzzing, some way behind the reach of these headlamps, but that pause turns to chaos.

'What is it?' I yell, sprinting for the ridge now. I feel my heart begin to hammer, but ignore the plea from Denis to start up the truck. We cannot afford to lose this prize. I will not let my brother down.

'Dune buggies!' Lena switches her gun one way then the other, as if unsure which one to take out first.

'Don't shoot!' I urge her. 'Save the bullets!'

Firing at a moving vehicle is a waste of time. Now that I knew what was coming, I also didn't want to bait the devils behind it. Only one crew rides that kind of vehicle out here, which is why Lena had called out so decisively.

'They're coming this way!' she shouts as I scramble towards her. 'Alexi, we must act!'

Our rivals, the Molotov Horde, belong to no fishing village, lost resort or harbour. This loose collective haunt the steppes to the north, in a convoy of trailers, buggies, camels, motorbikes and trucks. They never stay in the same place for more than a month. Many of them have roots in Mongolia, to the far east beyond the mountains, and are here to harvest rocket parts, just like us. This horde is a hardy bunch, with a reputation for brutality when things don't go their way. One time they showed up at the market behind our apartment block, and people just melted away. These guys are older than us by some years, mostly in their early twenties, and so we steer clear of them at every opportunity. We aren't dumb. We want to survive. We also know that one day our time will come. They have age and strength on their side, but we are the new blood with speed and stealth on ours. We were at the crash site first, after all, but that doesn't count for much when I look around me now.

'Everybody follow me!' I have to raise my voice to be heard, half expecting a cloud of hornets to fall upon us at any moment. I'm midway between the rocket and the sand bar, in the pool of light from our search lamp, but it's clear that I can't reach Lena in time. I come to a halt, thinking it would be better to appear ready for them now than be caught running around like hens. The twins rush to join me, and I am grateful to be flanked by them. I glance around for the others, only to see someone taking cover in the gloom behind the booster.

'Don't be cowards,' I shout at my crew, wherever they might be. 'We have to stand together!'

'Too late,' mutters Maxim, the elder twin. 'We're on our own.'

I can't blame them for being so alarmed, I tell myself. In some ways I am relieved that my brother has gone to ground with them. Just so long as nobody does anything stupid, there is still a chance we will get out of here alive.

I call out to Lena. She doesn't turn from her post this time. I just hope that she can hear me. 'Go easy with your trigger finger,' I instruct her. 'The Bat and I can sort this out.'

I had come across the Horde's main man on many occasions. Baatarsaikhan rarely came out in daylight, so it seemed fitting to shorten his name. You only have to take one look at him to know he prefers it this way. Usually our encounters went like this: we would arrive first at a smouldering rocket or satellite, and then make a swift getaway if the Molotov Horde showed up. Sometimes we would circle back in the truck to trade insults, but The Bat and I always exchanged a private salute. I sometimes think he has respect for me as a salvager, but will never show it because to him I am just a kid.

'We're sitting targets!' This is Anton. He sounds freaked, which speaks volumes.

'It's madness staying here,' Maxim chimes in. 'We're facing psychopaths.'

'The Bat was our age one time,' I remind them, but any further reassurance falls away when the first vehicle springs over the ridge.

The dune buggy roars in at an angle, slicing down the slope in front of Lena. Then another one scissors in from her other side. No more follow, which is some relief, though it also tells me this is only the scouting party. 'Be cool,' I hiss over my shoulder, though I can't even be sure that anyone is with me any more. I say it again, however, if only to assure myself.

The first buggy has pulled up right in front of me. I am dazzled by the lamps on the roll bar and the fender, but refuse to shield my eyes or look away. I don't even want to risk swallowing in case it betrays a hint of fear. I just grit my teeth and hope my legs don't give way. The driver guns the engine to test me, and then kills it. The headlamps go out, but I'm left so dazzled that all I see is a dark shape behind the wheel. I sense that whoever it is must be looking beyond me, at the space wreck shining under our own lights. Then this figure in the cockpit speaks, and I know for sure that I'm facing the top man.

'Now *that* is what I call a prize from the skies! I can see why you stuck around, Alexi. She's terrific! Congratulations, my friend.'

The Bat climbs out of his buggy, snaps off his goggles and comes around to shake my hand. He has a broad, weather-beaten face and a shallow nose, the mark of a true Mongolian. He is only a little bit taller than me, but his confidence outshines my own. I struggle to match his grip, and I can see it in his smile. He is wearing a trench coat with leather toggles and a Soviet storm trooper's helmet. He tips it back now with one finger, still sizing up the booster rocket.

'We found it first,' I say, struggling to sound as cool and calm. 'It's ours, this time.'

'Are you suggesting some kind of rule?' He gives me this side-on look, as if unsure he has heard me right. I try to find my voice so I can repeat myself, but he's already moved on. 'Did you see her drop? It was something, wasn't it? We would've been here an hour ago, but the towing tractor took a puncture.'

'I'm serious,' I say again, determined not to be toyed with here. 'This one belongs to us.'

Ignoring me still, The Bat summons the second driver. He's wearing the same kind of goggles, which he doesn't remove when he crosses the sand so his boss can mutter instructions. I hear something about radioing co-ordinates, which makes me wonder how much longer we have here. I feel as if he's treating me like some stupid child. My cheeks heat up and I even sense my vision swim. *If I cry*, I think to myself, *I'm finished.*

'Will you listen to me?' I snap at Baatarsaikhan, surprising even myself. It's enough to break up their conversation, and I am shocked to realise that I also have his full attention again. 'You have to let us take care of this one,' I continue, quieter now. 'Any other time, I swear, we'll leave it alone.'

'I don't believe I'm hearing this.' The Bat sounds impatient all of a sudden, his true nature coming through. 'Kid, my advice is to leave before the others show up. Some of my crew really don't like you, Alexi. They say you're growing too big for your boots. I can't stop them from spanking your behind if they feel you should be punished.'

The second driver seems to find this amusing as he heads back to his buggy. He reaches in to unclip the radio handset, still chuckling to himself. I look at The Bat once more, and find his pale pinched eyes waiting for me. There's no smirk held in check this time, no hint that he's fooling around. He takes a step closer, finding my ear like some kind of conspirator. 'Why don't you come back later?' he suggests under his breath. 'Take what's left behind.'

'The scraps?' I spring away, furious now. 'What do you take us for? Man, we found it first! You got as far as a burst tractor tyre. That tells me maybe *you're* on the way out. Face it—'

'That's enough!' The Horde leader squares up to me now, and I realise with a start that I've pushed him too far. 'How dare you disrespect me?' he spits in my face, and then shoves me hard in the chest with both hands. I cry out, backing away now, but it's clear that The Bat has only just begun. 'I was offering you a deal, fool. A chance to get out of here with some pride. Now you'll have to pay!'

6

I am aware of the dagger just as soon as he rounds on me. There it is under his trench coat, in a sheath attached to his belt. I had thought it was there for show because it looks Arabian, almost antique. Now his palm curls around the grip, and the world seems to slow to a halt.

'Don't you dare! Don't even think about it!' The voice pipes up from behind him, furious and determined, but it doesn't belong to my gunman. The Bat spins around, his trench coat swirling. Then I see Misha behind him, coming out of the dark with the crowbar. My brother looks like he's about to strike a baseball, the way he's braced. 'I swear I'll crack your skull wide open if you so much as touch him! This is *our* rocket, just like he told you the first time!'

The Bat abandons the dagger as instructed, but at the same time he appeals for some help. When his second driver fails to answer, I look around for him and immediately sense some relief. For there he is, beside the buggy, but with both hands held high like his boss. I see the radio handset in the sand and a pistol snub pressed to his neck.

'No sudden moves,' Lena calls across to us, and I wish

that I had seen her creep up on the guy. 'I took that opportunity,' she adds, 'and look what happened to your buddy here. Now listen to Mish and leave us alone.'

The Bat returns to face me, still amused despite it all. 'The Crowbar Kid here is your brother?' He raps his knuckles on the lip of his helmet. 'The one with the bomb in his head?' I am not surprised that he is wise to Misha's condition. There is little that the Molotov Horde do not know, which is why they hold such power in the region. 'It's a terrible shame,' he goes on, but what he says next shocks me to the core. 'The kind of news that would probably finish off Papa Titov, right?'

'You know Yasha?'

I glance at Mish, see him frozen in the background. He still has the iron cranked behind him, but I wonder if he might let it drop to the sand at what he just heard. The Bat knows way too much about us both, but we can handle ourselves. Now it seems that his knowledge stretches to what remains of our family, and I don't like that one bit.

'Our fathers go *way* back,' The Bat crows next, clearly unconcerned by Misha now. 'When my pa first arrived here, he used to do some trade at the docks as a sideline to the rockets. A small black-market operation trading motor oil for vodka and tobacco. Nothing that would cause anyone trouble, until Yasha found out about it.' He stops there for a second, clearly simmering. 'Who did he think he was, forbidding that kind of trade from taking place?'

'He was posted in the harbour office,' I remind him,

aware of the standards he kept. 'It was his job to keep all harbour business shipshape.'

'My father offered to make it worth his while to turn a blind eye.'

'And *my* father would not be bribed! He's a man of principle. Always will be!'

The Bat just grins for a second, as if my loss of cool is his victory this time. 'It's what his principles cost us that concerns me, Alexi. My family certainly managed, despite the penalty fine, but they had to make sacrifices. It's the sort of thing you never forget.' He stops there and jerks a thumb at my brother, not smiling any more. 'Especially times like now.'

'Forget about our fathers,' snaps Misha, weighing the crowbar once again. 'This is between us, not them. Now get out of here, *deegeneeraatsin*!'

The Bat shoots me another look, like I really ought to control my kid brother's tongue at the very least. He is a formidable presence, even with his buddy under guard, but there's no menace in it for me any more. I look at Misha again and realise that it all boils down to courage. The rest of my crew seem to have recognised this, too. Those who hid away when the buggies burst in on us are beginning to creep out into the open. It makes me think we can really pull this off. I look around me now, taking stock of everyone. When I see my rival do likewise, I repeat my brother's demand.

'Take a good look at us,' I add, stepping up now with my heart in my mouth. 'We might be kids to you, but if you want to see what we can do, just say the word.'

'How old are you? Fourteen?'

'Sixteen,' I am pleased to correct him, and then dare to point out that most of the others are younger, except for the girl holding his man hostage over there. 'Lena turns my age this winter, but already I trust her with my life. That's why she gets to take care of the pistol. I only have to say the word and my gunhand with your friend there will use it, no question.' Lena shifts her weight from one foot to the other. She still has the gun pressed to the poor guy's throat, but neither take their eyes off The Bat for a blink. I sense more movement behind me. My crew, regrouping, I hope and pray. We may not amount to much, but it's still a show of strength with everything we had. I concentrate on breathing steadily, desperate not to let him see how shook up I really am. Misha seems quite calm by comparison, though the crowbar in his hands tells me he has never been more certain about something in his life.

Baatarsaikhan turns slowly through all this, considering us all.

'So what do you say now?' I ask, when he meets my eyes once more. I feel those clear, almost see-through orbs lock onto me, as if memorising every last detail.

'Alexi,' he says finally. 'I'd say you're dead already.'

As if in response, a sound cuts through the night air behind me like a sheet snapping open. I turn with a start, to find Denis with the cutting equipment. He waits for the flame to brighten and build, his spectacles like circles of light now, and then shows the tip to the Mongol. 'You want me to go to work, boss? We're wasting time here.'

I can't be sure if he's talking about the rocket or our rival, but then there's nothing more I can say. The Bat shifts his attention to me once again, and holds it there for what seems like an age. Finally, he offers me his hand. We shake once more, only this time I return his grip. Once I let go he forms his fingers into an imaginary pistol, which he fires at me one time.

'It's all yours, Alexi. Be lucky. And be quick as well. It isn't just the military who might track you down now.'

Baatarsaikhan makes sure he scopes out every one of us as he retreats to his buggy, his stare lingering for longest on my little brother. I tell Lena she can stand down now, which she does without question. The second driver breathes out hard, rubbing his neck, like the gun muzzle had just branded him, until his boss barks at him to be a man and get a grip. The Bat is the first to start his engine, and I know before he hits the gas hammer that he's going to head straight through us. My crew are ready too, and open up a path. The two vehicles peel apart in front of the rocket, before throttling around for the sand bar and the endless dark beyond.

'We did it!' Misha is the first to clench a fist in victory. The others take a second or so to realise that the rocket really is ours to claim, and then turn to each other in glee. I smile and cheer with them, but from the sidelines now. Only Lena seems to share my reservations. She accepts a cigarette from me. When I strike a match for her, she dips over it with her eyes on me.

'They'll be back, Alexi, and in force.'

'I know that. We must work now as if our lives depend on it.'

'Our lives *do* depend on it,' she points out, and turns her attention to my kid brother. Misha is still dancing down there in the pool of light, the centre of attention for once. 'Do you think he knows what he just did back then?'

'He's a courageous kid,' I agree.

'Frankly, I think you're both cracked,' she tells me. 'Nobody faces off The Bat. *Nobody*.'

'It had to be done eventually.' I stub out my smoke early, anxious now for everyone to return to work. I also want to hide my hands so she doesn't see that I am trembling. 'Even if it does mean there's a price to pay,' I add to finish, 'we did the right thing.'

7

We slip inside our apartment at sunrise. If I shut my eyes now, the smell of mould and stale incense would still tell me I am home. Even the sounds are familiar and reassuring, from the wind breathing in through the warped window frame to the wall clock that ticked too slow. It used to be that you could hear the neighbours on either side, as well as above and below. The place was built to house six hundred families, but many have moved out. The way I see it, those who remain are too sick, stupid or stubborn to leave.

Our father's bedroom door is shut, but there is no way of knowing whether he is asleep. Over the years, his sense of time has slipped from his grip until day or night makes no difference to him. He simply dozes whatever the hour, and not always in his bed. Sometimes we can find him in his chair overlooking the desert scrub, so lost in thought or deep in dreams that he appears at first to have stopped breathing.

'Alexi, I'm hungry.'

'*Shh!*' I press my finger to my lips and direct my brother into the kitchen. There are no windows in here. The only light comes from a bare light bulb. On the shelf above the sink are jars containing rice, lentils, preserved fruits and pickles. Fresh food is hard to find, and even if we can find a source it's likely to be poisoned. I have a soft spot for crunching on raw carrots, just like my mother who first shared some with me. Lately, however, we have been advised by the authorities to lop off three inches from each end as a precaution against herbicide and radiation in the soil. It leaves little more than a mouthful, and what is the point in that? If my mother were here she would ignore the warnings. She'd also have this kitchen stocked against the odds.

'I'm starving.' Misha dips down to search the old fridge. He picks through the shelves, coming back with a plate of dried, cured meat cuts, a pot of lumpy yoghurt and a crinkled-up nose. 'This is no way to finish work,' he whispers. Then he grins at me, and I can't help but do the same thing. It's been a long night, but one that has paid off handsomely. 'Forget the fridge,' he says next, and springs back to his feet. 'At this hour we can be at the market when it opens.'

'Let's get out of here,' I agree, thinking, at least we can afford to eat well for once. I turn to leave, only to find my father right there in the frame.

'My sons,' says Yasha, as if reminding himself who we are. He is dressed in loose cotton trousers, a collarless shirt and shawl, but I can't be sure if he has just woken up or come home right after us. He just stands there looking unfocused, rubbing at his bristles.

'Did you see the lift-off yesterday?' he asks next. 'It was a thing of beauty, boys. If anyone was out there to pick up the pieces, my guess is they'll be rich this morning.'

Overnight, our crew had made two hundred bucks from breaking up the booster. We had loaded the truck with as much as it would carry, and then radioed our middleman with good news. As ever, the trade-off was a shady, scary business. I didn't like it one bit. We had arrived at an outpost of his choice, not ours. It was somewhere near the oil fields, because we could see tongues of fire on the horizon where the rigs were burning off. The place was little more than a huddle of run-down tin shacks and a stable with a door that kept banging in the breeze. It may have once belonged to cattle drovers, only now it was crawling with men in quilted jackets, and sunglasses, despite the dark. Some of them carried sub-machine guns, and could've cut us down in seconds if they wished. Our man had appeared out of nowhere. He was dressed in a pale linen suit with a shirt wide open at the throat, and spoke in an accent that always made me think he came a long way for this line of business. Having ordered someone pick over the metal on the wagon, he then offered me a price that very nearly made me whistle.

The deal was never normally so generous. Usually, the fear that we might not make it home alive would persuade me to settle on his first offer. What happened this time was different. I knew for sure that we had a lot of precious metal to show, as well as some of the motor parts that Denis had managed to salvage. So, he had offered me one hundred and seventy-five bucks – but this time I held out. Not just for my brother's sake, but because my crew had faced down The Bat, and I wanted to reward them in the only way that mattered. Our man didn't like it one bit. Even so, when he counted out the cash he grudgingly admitted we had come into our own of late. We might've been kids, he said, but we were courageous and, more importantly, we were here with the merchandise.

At last, we were delivering goods matched by nobody else. Our big break had finally arrived, and now here I was making plans to walk away from it all. My brother's health gave me no other choice. I would leave the salvaging business without hesitation, if it meant Mish could be well again. Only one thing threatens to hold us back, and that becomes clear right now in our apartment. For I look into my father's tired, hollow eyes, and wonder how on earth he would survive without us.

'Papa,' I say gently, feeling trapped in this kitchen all of a sudden. 'That rocket you saw? Mish and I chased down the booster. It was us. *We* found it.'

'You did?' He seems confused at first, but then shrugs like he couldn't be expected to keep track of us, anyhow. Yasha has a good heart, but if I were to leave him in charge of Misha they'd never wash their faces or clothes. 'You should be grateful that the tide hasn't shown up yet and claimed that kind of treasure. Mark my words, it'll come in one day and take us all by surprise.'

'Sure it will,' I say, just to keep him sweet. 'In time, Papa.'

'We were just going to the market to celebrate,' my

brother says, sounding as bright as ever. 'We even beat the Horde—'

'Mish!' I shoot a look to silence him, but it's too late for that. Our father may exist in his own private world much of the time, but he hadn't cut himself off from us completely. He turns to me now, his brow lifting. 'The Molotov Horde,' I explain. 'They were chasing the same thing as us.'

'Those are crazy boys!' He clacks his tongue. 'From a crazy family.'

'So is it true?' This is Misha once again, all lit up at the wrong time. He turns and looks up at me. 'What The Bat said about our fathers crossing swords? Did that really happen?'

'Not now!' I caution him under my breath, but it's too late. I may be anxious to avoid troubling Yasha in any way, but he has clearly registered what Mish just said. It leaves me no choice but to smile casually and attempt to play things down. 'What happened is history,' I tell my brother, speaking up to be sure that Yasha hears me, too. 'Am I right, Papa?'

He nods, absently, but it is clear that he is lost as ever in some memory from the past. Finally, he clears his throat and says: 'Promise you won't mess with the Molotov Horde any more. They hold grudges, believe me, and I don't want my boys in trouble.'

'It's a little late for that,' I say sheepishly, and glare at my brother for forcing the issue so soon. I know I have to tell Yasha that Mish and I will soon be going away for a while, but I don't feel ready just yet. 'Papa, it's been a long night. We really have to eat and then think about sleep.'

Our father nods as if he understands, and leans against the sink to let us pass. As I leave the kitchen he claps me on the shoulder. I turn to look up at him, find his eyes are shining up. I think for a moment he might say something. His lower lip is trembling, but no words follow and I know he won't let those tears fall in front of us. 'Everything will be just fine,' I tell him. 'Trust me.'

8

Misha buys two honey pastries from the market. There isn't much else on offer. Indeed, the fresh food has almost all gone. Like the sea, the number of traders here has shrunk over time. We're in a square behind the big old cannery. The sun clips the roof up there, throwing light onto a scattering of stalls and half-empty animal pens. There's a smell of cow dung and tobacco in the air, while the camel tethered under the archway to the harbour is making more noise than all the cattle and the hens put together. I hang back from my kid brother as he pays for the pastries, and wonder how this scene would've played out half a century before. More people would've been here, with more spring in their step, more noise, some laughter, and the heady smell of freshly-caught fish.

We eat our breakfast on the old harbour wall, sitting with our legs over the edge. An uneven trail runs along the wall, just beneath our feet. It's silvery in colour, and about an inch thick. The old stevedores who once shouldered giant sturgeon from ship to shore will say it's a tidewater mark. The stonework below is darker, but in my view a lot of it has clearly been caused by rot and decay.

'Do you think he'll manage without us?' asks Mish. I know who he's talking about because I've been dwelling on the very same thing: Papa.

'We could bring him along for the ride,' I say. 'But it would mean telling him about your treatment.'

'Then he should be told.' My brother tears a mouthful from his pastry. 'You keep saying it's nothing to worry about, after all.'

I pick at my teeth, squinting into the wind. Your eyes can sting if you stay in the same place too long, and that's all down to the salt. It swirls and drifts and claws across the landscape, as if searching for some place to settle. Somewhere beyond the horizon line I'm looking at lies the Baikonur cosmodrome – a launch complex belonging to the Russians, on soil leased from our government. The land is no good to anyone else, is what people say. It can't hold down roots of any kind, which is perhaps why the fortune that must have been made from such a deal isn't ploughed back into the region. I kick my heels against the sea wall, watch the brick dust crumble, and remind myself that it's just the way things are. I can't change how life is for us, but without the cosmodrome we would never be sitting here, contemplating our own flight out.

'Let me talk to Papa,' I say, sheltering behind my free hand now. 'But you have to swear you won't open your big mouth when I'm speaking. Seriously, Mish, I really don't think it's healthy for Yasha to know that we messed with the Horde last night.'

'Sorry.'

'Damn right you should be sorry!' I'm only playing at

54

being angry with him here, but as I speak I sense myself bristling. Looking out for us both could be tough enough at the best of times. Now I had to consider our father, as well as watch our backs. 'I'm sorry that we faced off with those devils in the first place,' I explain. 'We're marked men now, Mish, and that isn't right at our age.'

'But we're leaving,' he says, his voice pitched high.

'Leaving is one thing,' I agree. 'The question is: can we come back?'

Neither of us speaks for a moment, but in that time I realise that this place might actually mean something to me. Aral may offer nothing, but it's been my home for sixteen years. Now that we're close to heading out, even in a bid to help my brother get well, I still don't like the feeling it brings.

'I'm sorry, Mish,' I mutter finally. 'What I just said—'

'I know,' he cuts in, trying hard not to sound hurt. 'You always do the best for us, Alexi, and I just cause trouble.'

'Hey,' I say to silence him. 'You're never trouble.'

'But we wouldn't be in this situation if it wasn't for me.'

I figure he is talking about his health. I also realise it isn't something we can talk about in detail. It's a situation, just like he says. A situation that will be sorted.

'Let's just leave it that we need each other,' I suggest, rolling my shoulders to loosen up some. 'Take last night. What you did was foolish, but it showed real courage. Everyone is proud of you, little brother. Not just me.'

'It wasn't so much,' he says with a shrug. We glance at one another, the pair of us feeling goofy and stupid. Mish

55

reaches for the back of his head, burying his fingers into that shock of black hair. 'Can we stop talking about it, please?'

'Whatever you say, little brother.'

'I say, let's eat!'

We finish our pastries, listening to the wind singing through the cables on the stranded trawler down there. It rises and falls, but never rests or fades away. The sky over the seabed is pale and blue, scored by vapour trails from planes high overhead. I have never wondered where they come from or where they might be heading, until now. Finally, Misha yawns. It's infectious, I find, which is no surprise after such a long night.

'Come on,' I say. 'It's time we got out of here.' Now he turns to face me, looking uncertain somehow. His wide eyes don't leave me for a moment, and then I realise why. 'I'm saying let's go *home*, idiot! Back to our block. We won't be leaving for the city just yet. You can't just launch out of here, Mish. It takes preparation, just like it does for the rockets.'

My brother climbs to his feet, a flake of pastry clinging momentarily to one corner of his mouth. He looks tired, and not just from lack of sleep.

'Once I'm well again,' he says next, 'will we ever come back?'

'Of course!' I say, quick to sound upbeat. 'Where else is there?'

We turn for home, drifting between the harbour buildings with the wind behind us at last.

* * *

Little Disney is our name for the playground in the shadow of our block. All the kids call it that, as do the adults. It's been there for years, outlasting the joke. The seesaw and the roundabout could sorely use some oil, while the swings are as rusty as the ships. You just have to look at the chains to know that you ride on one at your own peril. Before I started taking care of Mish, however, I learned you could have a lot of fun if you were prepared to take the risk. The way it creaked and groaned, it was hard to shake off the fear that something very bad could happen. The only way to make the most of it was to hope that your turn would be over before the worst occurred. Among my crew, Lena is the first to get on and the last to get off, so it's no surprise to find her reaching for the early stars later that afternoon.

'Alexi!' she shouts as I cross the playground, tucking in her long legs as the swing plunges from its peak. The twins are out as well, sharing a bag of sunflower seeds and scuffing at the dust. Denis is with them, as are some of the younger kids left in the block. One of them looks a little retarded, kind of sloppy in the face. A lot of little ones have been born with more problems than most of us lately, but there's only one crazy who concerns me now and she's taking the swing to its limit. 'Two dollars and I'll jump!'

'What kind of example is that?' I kick at a crushed drink can, recover my step with my hands in my pockets. 'Anyway, you don't need the money after what we just earned ourselves.'

'So screw the money! Watch me fly!'

I'm just yards from Lena when she lets go on the upswing and spreads her arms wide. I really didn't think she would do it with me this close. All I can really take in is four limbs and one wide-open face bearing down on me. I throw my hands out defensively, but there's no stopping her now. The impact knocks the air from my lungs, and leaves her sprawled across me.

'*Ket kirpai!*' I curse in the dust, half laughing all the same. 'What do you think I am? Your safety net?' Lena coughs and giggles, and then buries her face into the pit of my shoulder. It's then that I hear some of the others teasing us, and realise why she's hiding. I feel my cheeks heat, and do my best to push her off.

'What's the matter?' squeaks one of the grunts. 'Scared she might kiss you?'

'He loves her!' chimes another. '*Alexi loves Lena!*'

I ease myself onto my elbows, some pain in my back still from the impact, and scowl at the girl standing over me. She grins sheepishly and offers me her hand. I tell her I can manage myself, just like I always have. 'One day a stunt like that is going to get you killed!'

'So I meet my maker with some cash for once!' She keeps her hand outstretched, and then grabs my own as I struggle upright. 'Not that I can take the money with me, but I'd go knowing what fun it was fleecing those Molotov monkeys.'

'Don't joke,' I warn, brushing myself down. 'Next time we head across the seabed, my guess is they'll be waiting for us.'

'Maybe so,' she says, with a shrug like she couldn't care

less any longer. 'But it was still beautiful, what your brother did.'

'Where is Misha?' This is Denis, the only one who hadn't crowed over what had just happened. He crosses the concrete to join us, his hands tucked inside his seat pockets. With his glasses and his closely-cropped hair he looks like the sort of kid you'd find sitting at the front of a class. He's a smart boy, too, so it's a shame that he no longer has that opportunity. Like most things here, our education slowly fell apart as families continued to leave. I heard the old schoolhouse is still open, but there's been no point showing up ever since the last few teachers moved out too. I tell Denis that my brother is sleeping still, and that he needs it more than most.

'Don't take this the wrong way,' Lena warns me, sounding serious now. 'But sometimes I think you worry too much. The kid can take care of himself, like he showed us all.'

'She's right.' Denis pauses to pop a sunflower seed into his mouth. He chews on it, spits the husk into the dust. 'You need to loosen up, Alexi. Taking Misha out of here for treatment is a good thing, but you can't be responsible for him every second of his day. He has to live a little.'

'If someone doesn't watch out for him,' I say, feeling stung all of a sudden, 'he may not live at all! You both know he can have a moment at any time. God alone knows what might happen if I wasn't there to make sure he's safe. The only time I feel I can leave Mish is when he's asleep – away from any excitement. I don't feel I have to spend it by justifying myself to you.'

'Hey, easy!' Lena shows me her palms, pats the air – like this might calm me down. 'We all want the best for your brother. We also want the best for you.' She looks to Denis for support, who flattens his lips and nods at me.

'I can take care of myself.' I look from Lena to Denis and back again, and then grin because I really don't want to fall out with my friends. 'But who's going to look after you goons when I'm gone?'

Denis smiles and chips at the seed husk with his foot. 'When are you planning to leave?' he asks. I tell him maybe next week. Once I've broken the news to our father, taken care of the truck, and made sure both won't be neglected when I'm gone. Lena wants to know what station will take us to the old capital, and whether our travel papers are in order. I answer all their questions, aware that we're just going through the motions here. What I really want to say to my friends goes unspoken. I'll miss them all, but can't begin to find the words because I've never been without them. If this is the first of my goodbyes, I think to myself, it's tougher than I had thought.

'You know what I won't miss?' I say brightly, anxious now to move on from this moment. I gesture at the block behind them. It's ten storeys high, built from concrete and steel, with balconies on every floor. There are three blocks in all: this one and two behind it, arranged like dominoes set to fall. That's how the residents describe them. I have always thought of them as tombstones, and tell my friends just that.

'There's no place like home,' says Lena dryly. 'Even if nothing ever happens here.'

For a beat we study this soulless slab of Soviet architecture. The wind has dropped now that dusk is here, the bluster gone out of the day. It's as close to silence as we can ever hope to get – a slowed-down kind of peace that comes to an end with the sound of glass popping.

With a start, I see flames flash from one of the upper windows. Then comes the blast, spitting debris through smoke.

At first I think a bucketful of water is spreading through the air up there. Then Lena yells for the kids to get away and I realise that I'm looking at falling glass.

'Move!' I shout across at them, as the first shards begin to strike the dust. I see the twins grab the kids and scatter, hear one of them screaming and then some shouting from the block. I look up again, locate the smashed and blackened frame, and feel my heart heave when my brother's face appears in it.

'Alexi!' he cries out, sounding choked and panic-stricken. 'Where are you, brother? God help us, *come quick!*'

9

A grenade had gone off in our apartment. That much I learn as I rush from the playground. I hear Mish scream that they had come looking for me, and already I know who's behind it. All I can think is that we're on the cusp of darkness. A time when bats take wing.

I sprint through the space between two of the blocks, onto the dirt road facing the desert. A string of telegraph poles runs along the far side of the road, some of them skewed out of line. I follow them left and then right, see no sign of life, and then my eyes fall upon the swirl of tyre tracks outside our building. Lena is right beside me now, along with Denis and the twins. Somebody curses and points out across the seabed. At this hour, the light is little more than a burnt-orange band on the horizon. Great pools of shadow have begun to fill every depression in the expanse ahead. It's hard to follow the tracks, the way they come and go, but then, fading into the distance, I can just make out that all too familiar drone.

'Sons of bitches,' breathes Denis. 'This is a *war*.'

Dune buggies have been here, but they're too far away now to chase. Without a word, I break from my crew and rush for the entrance. I don't care if the Molotov Horde make a clean getaway this time. My only concern is the devastation that's been left behind.

'Alexi, they came and went so fast!'

Little Mish is on the landing, waiting for me. He looks paler than ever, standing there in his vest and pants. The door to our apartment has been kicked open, I see, and an acrid smoke hangs in the air. I grip my kid brother by his shoulders and look him in the eyes. 'Where is Papa?' I ask, dreading what I might expect.

'They didn't come for him.'

'But is he hurt?'

Mish shakes his head, blinking back tears. 'They came for *us*, Alexi. Just bust their way inside, lobbed a grenade into our bedroom and left as it went off.'

'Are you hurt?' I ask.

'Only in my ears.'

'I should have never left you, Mish. What happened?'

'I was in the bathroom, taking a pee. I heard them coming in and cracked open the door so I could see. There were three of them, including Baatarsaikhan. I saw him good and, for a moment, I thought he had seen me. Then Papa came into the hallway to confront them. They warned him to back off, pulled the pin to show they weren't fooling around, and told him they had come to wake us up. It was a flash grenade, thank God.'

'How do you know?'

'Look at me,' he says, and spreads his arms. 'I'm still alive.'

I feel an odd sense of relief when he says this. A flash grenade could scare you half to death, maybe, but it was all noise and smoke. If a crate ever found its way onto the black market, you could be sure the tearaways in the area would have plenty to entertain themselves with for a few days afterwards.

'Did they say anything more?'

'Just that they would be back.'

Mish stops there, as if waiting for me to make everything better. All I can do is look away. I feel as if I have let my brother down. He may have humiliated Baatarsaikhan out on the seabed, but I started this thing. I had asked my crew to stand together, and by rights I should've taken steps to defend and protect. I had expected the Horde to strike back, of course, but the success of our salvage had distracted me from really doing anything about it. Now we had funds, my thoughts had turned to Misha's treatment, at a time when we should've gone to ground. What The Bat had done was ruthless, but just the way things were. There is no room for competition out here, with so little means to survive. We had challenged the order of things, and naturally they were retaliating – by hitting us harder than anyone could've imagined.

Denis and the twins arrive on the stairs behind me now, along with the younger ones and some other residents.

'Where is Lena?' I ask, aware that she is not among them.

'Outside,' says Denis, and pats his hip as if he is the

one with the gun. 'Just in case anyone comes back to finish the job.'

I glance at those residents who have braved coming out, two *babushkas* and a woman with a bawling baby, and tell them our pressure cooker just blew up on us. They don't look like they believe me for one minute, especially the old grandmothers, but there are enough of us on the landing now to encourage them back to their apartments. At a time like this, I wish police still patrolled around here. The *militzia* would've persuaded The Bat to steer clear, but they only ever show up if a politician or press crew is in the region. Without that kind of presence in the harbour, all kids like us can do is act like tough guys and keep our terror to ourselves.

'You're shaking,' my brother says, once they're out of earshot. I realise I have been holding him by the wrists, and quickly hide my hands from him. I can feel myself trembling now, the shock of what has happened slowly kicking in, and my thoughts turn to our father.

'Stay here,' I say. 'Get your breath.'

'Why? I want to come with you.'

'Papa doesn't deserve any of this. All he deserves is an explanation, and that has to come from me.'

'You're going to tell him that we're leaving?'

'I'm going to tell him that we're *all* leaving, brother. At first light. It isn't safe here any more.'

I find Yasha in the main room. He's there in his chair, facing the window as always, with his hands clasped in his lap. He has his back to the damage from the blast, which

66

is impossible for me to ignore. I step over the blackened carpet in front of our bedroom, the smell like a spent firework, and wonder what must be going through his mind. This is our home. The one place in his world that hasn't changed over the years, until now.

'I am so sorry this has happened, Papa.' I pause to consider what I have to say, thinking about The Bat and what had gone down between our fathers all those years ago. 'I thought I could make a stand as you once had. It seems that I was wrong.'

He nods, just taking it in, but doesn't speak or turn to face me. I reach for the light switch, only to drop my hand away. He may be looking out at near darkness, but I sense he prefers it that way. Lights would only reflect the interior, and I didn't think he needed that now.

'I've seen many things from here,' he says finally, in such a murmur I have to come closer. 'Some terrible things, but also great beauty.'

'The sea,' I say with a sigh, thinking I have heard this so often. I really don't want to be here, picking over the past again, nor entertaining the hopeless belief that the tide might return. All I want to do is convince my father to come with us, but I know I can't just spring it on him. Not after the shock we've all just suffered. It's clear he's dazed, in fact, because his eyes don't fog at the very mention of his long-lost ocean.

'I must be honest, Alexi, I took Aral for granted when she was here. We all did. The year the water levels first began to drop, we were more concerned with how to fix the ice-maker in the cannery.'

'But everyone talks about the sea like it was liquid gold.' I drop down beside him, waiting for my moment.

'It really was, one time.' He turns to me now, and I realise he has something to tell me before I can begin to break my news to him. 'Whenever the Soviets tested an atomic bomb over the steppes, people for hundreds of miles around were instructed to turn away from the detonation. Even this far from the site, officials would show up in the square some days before and make sure we understood what to do when the siren sounded. I was young at the time, and headstrong like you, Alexi. I didn't like other people calling the shots for me. So, I ignored the advice and watched one go off from here.' Papa gestures into the gloom, gazing at some imaginary point now, far across the seabed. 'The way it bloomed on the horizon, I thought I was watching the crest of a second sun dawning. The sky appeared to darken, it was so intense.'

'You actually saw it detonate?'

'Even felt a little heat on my face,' he says, with what sounds like some pride. 'Had I hidden away I would've missed the light spread over the water. For a moment, it seemed like every ripple and wave had turned molten.' His lids fall just then, but I can't be sure if he is tormented by this memory or in awe of it. 'By the time I looked out across the sea again, the blast had given rise to a bloom of smoke and fire. It seethed and boiled and lifted and *blossomed*,' he adds breathlessly, conjuring the memory high with a gesture of his hands. 'The testing grounds may have been several days' journey from here, but some of the shapes summoned in that furnace made me think I had witnessed both heaven and hell. I saw angels and I saw spectres, my boy, right from this very window.' He drifts off again there, having been so fired up, and settles back in his chair. 'Only a turn in the tide could take my breath away now, no matter what else comes across the sands.'

I figure he is talking about the dune buggies, because he stops there and faces me. I wonder if he knew they had shown up for us, despite doing nothing to sound the alarm. If so, it seems my father is simply waiting for death.

'Papa,' I say, angered now that he could feel so defeated. 'We cannot stay here any more. We should have gone before Mama died. Look around you. Open your eyes! It's going to get us all *killed*, and I will not stand back and let that happen. Not to you, not to Misha, not to me. We're family, Papa.'

'And this is our home!' He smashes one fist into his palm, startling me. I hadn't realised he was capable of such emotion still. 'Do you think a bunch of punks are going to drive me out after all the shit that has happened here?'

'Those punks are just the half of it,' I say, seizing my moment. 'The Molotov Horde will be back, just like they said, but that isn't the only reason why we have to move on. Papa, there is something you have to know.'

I fall silent, aware that I have his full attention now. I am unsure how to tell him that his younger son is gravely ill, to soften the impact somehow. I open a sentence by apologising, only to close it again. I draw breath to try a different way, but another voice speaks instead.

'He's leaving home for me.' I turn to see Misha himself. There in the hall. Others crowd behind him, checking out the blast damage, all of them curious about us. 'I'm sick, Papa. The moments I've been having aren't harmless. They're seizures, and they won't just go away as I grow up.'

'Don't say that,' whispers Yasha, out of nowhere it seems, and I wonder if he knew all along.

'You can't hide from the truth any more,' I say gently, and invite him to look around. 'And I can't protect you from it. Papa, it's no good just staring out of that window. The sea is gone. This land is dead. It's history, but we still have a future. Look at what's going on right here with your family, and then tell me you'll come too. We're heading for the old capital. They can help us there.'

He looks from me to little Mish, as if seeking some kind of second opinion. The kids behind him are torn between staring into the broken bedroom and the broken man beside me.

'Did you really see a mushroom cloud?' my kid brother asks.

It is Yasha who breaks the silence that follows by laughing. It comes out of nowhere, like a release that had to happen, and ceases just as abruptly. Even if it does sound like his way of holding back tears, I can't help smiling myself. 'I saw it with my very own eyes,' he confirms, staring into space again. It makes me think he is about to drift away once more. Instead, with a sigh, he rises from the chair. I follow him up myself, and know for sure that he is with us when he eases himself around to face the room at last. 'There are stories I can tell you, little Mish,' he adds, 'but it seems the only one that matters is happening right here and now.'

'Then leave with us,' I plead. 'And see it through to the end.'

10

People here drink for many reasons, but mostly to forget. That's how my mother used to explain it to me, whenever we saw a drunk slumped around the harbour. As a little boy, I could not understand why anyone would want to get themselves in such a state, and I still feel the same way now. Sure, I'd like to put a few things behind me, just like some of the old seafarers who drown their sorrows from daybreak, but the way I plan to do it means I won't wake up to the same desolation again.

'Alexi, here's to you.'

I accept the vodka bottle that comes my way and take a slug. The heat in my throat is intense, the alcohol as raw as it is cheap, but I'm ready for it. I drink like most other kids, but only in celebration. It doesn't matter how bleak the situation can be for us, there's always got to be something we can toast. I look around now, the sun lifting into my last morning here, and salute my crew with the bottle.

'There are few things I'm going to miss around here,' I say. 'But they all mean a great deal to me.'

I hand the vodka on, pleased that there is enough left for everyone. A chill wind is blowing from the north today, a sign that the seasons are changing, and so everyone welcomes the hit. I pull the sleeves of my sweater over my knuckles, wishing I had come out with my overcoat and cap, and join in the next toast.

The bottle goes around in a circle, each handover with a salute to the things that matter to us. We drink to the cosmodrome and her rockets, the specialists in Almaty who will cure little Mish, and not the return of the sea, of course, but its loss. Away to the north and west, the former coastline spreads out in mounds and ridges. Behind each one, you would expect to find the waterline, but from experience I know that you have to travel a long way before the terrain becomes boggy and finally wet. One time some years ago, Lena, Denis and I set off to see if we could find it for ourselves. It was a fun trek, to begin, but eventually the disappointment and frustration that increased with every rise persuaded us to give up. Even so, we toast it with great fondness, also the harbour and her inhabitants. We don't just drink to those who remain, but the people who have lived and died here. It's why I walked to the cemetery at first light, and where my crew caught up with me as I stood before my mother's grave.

'Will you be back?' This is Lena now. It's her turn to make the toast. The hot breath that carried her question turns white in the air. I watch it vanish, then tell her that first we need to find what we're looking for. She nods and drops her gaze, only to come back with the bottle held high. 'Wherever you go,' she says, and then cradles it to her chest, 'I'll always be right here.'

I am unsure if she means in the harbour or her heart,

but figure both mean just as much. Today, Lena has swept her hair back in a band. She has a full-moon face with smooth, flat cheeks and eyes that crease when she smiles at me now.

'Most probably we'll *all* be here,' says Maxim.

His brother, Anton, looks around at the surrounding gravestones. 'Some of us never leave.'

The cemetery is situated beside what used to be the coastal road. Now it's just another track that would be lost were it not for the electricity pylons and this plot, ringed by a picket fence. I don't come out here much. Even sacred things cannot escape the everlasting blast of salt, wind and sand. What stonework is still visible amid the drifts is worn and hard to read, but this morning I had found my mother's from memory. There, I had unscrewed the bottle cap in her memory, hoping she would forgive me for the upset I was causing.

That's when most of my crew had shown up, but they hung back until I was through.

Nearly every kid I know has loved ones buried here. It's the first place you go looking for someone if they can't be found in their homes or around the harbour. I doubt that any of the crew had even bothered to knock on my door. With blackened walls and a window we had boarded as best we could, the place is literally a bombsite. I was just too wired to sleep there – unlike my kid brother, which is why I had left him at daybreak with a note to be ready to leave on my return.

'May you find what you're looking for in Almaty.' This is Denis with the toast right now. He finishes the last of the vodka and then lobs the bottle over the picket fence. 'At least you won't have to watch your back out there.'

I shrug, feeling some guilt for leaving my crew to face the Horde without me. 'If anyone wants to come along for the ride,' I suggest, 'they only have to say the word.'

The twins glance at one another, but then shake their heads. I turn to Lena, but she won't meet my eyes. Denis chooses the same moment to dig deep for his cigarettes. I refuse his offer of a smoke, and instead stress that I'm serious. Everyone, I say, is welcome to join us on the journey ahead. This time, he speaks for them all: 'Alexi, you're taking your father and your brother. Our families are still here, in some shape or form. People who depend on us.'

'But what about The Bat?'

Denis draws on his cigarette, thinking about what I have said. 'If you don't get help for Misha then he's going to die. Unlike you, we can stay here. It won't be the same without you both, but at least we stand a chance of staying alive.'

I glance at Lena once again, and wonder whether she's holding back this morning as a cover for something else. When she does catch my eye, however, I am first to look away. For a moment, I think that everyone must have noticed. I half expect to be teased for it. Instead, the uncomfortable silence is broken by Lena herself.

'Isn't that your truck?' I look up to see her nod at something over my shoulder. The first thing I see when I turn around is a funnel of dust in the distance. It's coming from the harbour, but the vehicle it appears to be chasing is just too far away for me to say if it's mine. Someone comments on the speed it is travelling. Then I hear the air-horn blaring, and swear out loud.

My father owned the truck before me. When he worked at the harbour office, he used it to travel up this same coastal track to Aralsk – once a thriving seaport, and now good for nothing but the railroad out of the region. There he'd do business with ship engineers and fish exporters, until the deals dwindled along with the sea. I remember my mother was secretly relieved when he gave up on that journey altogether. She didn't think it was safe, driving with a dead foot over the brake. Watching him make his first journey since I picked up the keys, I am left feeling both immensely proud and terribly anxious.

'Seems Yasha drives faster than you,' observes Denis, drily, as the truck slides to a halt in front of the gates to the cemetery. The dust cloud overshoots, and then clears to reveal my father at the wheel. Under any other circumstances, this would seem like a triumph. As I had instructed Misha to wait for me back at the apartment, I feel nothing but anxiety at seeing him here. My little brother is first out of the cab, but I am there to meet him before his scuffed pumps hit the sand.

'It's Papa,' he says breathlessly, as if they have run all the way. I am about to press him further when Yasha leans across the bench and urges us both to climb aboard.

'What's the hurry?' I ask, when he throttles the engine.

'Get in. We must leave!'

'He has a bad feeling,' says Mish, under his breath. 'He

told me to roll whatever I could grab into a blanket, and then insisted that we head off right away.'

I look to the crew, who seem just as mystified, so I instruct my brother to hang back with the others and then join my father in the cab. It's unusual for me to see him outside the apartment. He looks younger in natural light, especially as he's shaved, but also more spooked and unsettled. It occurs to me that this is the first time he has ventured so far in years, possibly since our mother was buried here. I want to think this means my father has conquered his demons, but the look on his face tells me otherwise.

'I'm really pleased to see you out here again,' I say, anxious not to agitate him further, 'but don't you think it might be safer if I did the driving?'

I notice that he's gripping the wheel as if the whole world might flip over at any moment. He doesn't even seem to register when I lean across and kill the engine.

'I've seen some things,' he says weakly, his knuckles whitening for a beat.

'I know that,' I reply, and gently remind him of our conversation the evening before. I assume his account of the atomic test had slipped his tired and traumatised mind. Then his eyes turn to mine, and I realise I may have misjudged him.

'These things,' he says, with more certainty this time. 'What I've seen has yet to happen.'

My first thought is that at least it makes a change from being troubled by his past. I just doubt telling him this would come as much comfort. The way he reads my expression, as if fearing some kind of ridicule, it leaves me with no choice but to nod and say, 'Go on.'

'It happened at first light,' he says, relaxing his grip on the wheel a little, 'as I watched the stars go out one by one.'

'You were dozing in your chair when I left,' I said. 'Maybe you dreamed it.'

'I haven't dreamed for years,' he says, quite certainly. 'Alexi, I heard you slip out, but it was only afterwards that I sensed it.'

'What?'

'Something terrible, like a dark storm gathering just beyond the horizon.'

'The Molotov Horde?' I want to assure him that my crew are the very best, with spirits hammered into shape by the elements – just like the gravestones behind me. They'll survive, and even live in peace when Baatarsaikhan accepts that we have gone. But I can sense my father may take some convincing. 'Winter will take care of everything,' I promise him. 'Fighting the cold is the biggest battle of all, for us and for the Horde.'

Yasha thinks about this and then shakes his head. 'The Horde are just the beginning,' he says darkly. 'The last time I felt this dread the sea was here and a nuclear warhead was about to set the sky on fire. I've never forgotten that sense of fear and expectation, which is why I can't ignore it now.' He turns in his seat to face me squarely: 'Something is going to go off, Alexi. Something bigger than a bomb, and far more certain than the return of the sea. I don't know what it is, but we have to do something. My boy, I wished the tide would wash in and take our troubles away, but you made me realise that's never going to happen. Now I've come to accept it, I cannot sit back and let another tragedy befall my family.'

'It's why I need to get little Mish out of here,' I explain. 'All I want is for him to live.'

'I'm thinking of you both,' says Yasha, and his eyes begin to shine once more. 'Now say your farewells and call your brother. There's a train to be caught.'

11

It feels strange to be on the passenger side of the bench. Stranger still is the sight of my village outpost shrinking in the truck's wing-mirror. For I just don't know when I'll see it again. I lean out of the window for one last, long look, and wave madly at my crew until the dust and the distance prove too much. My eyes are streaming when I come back in, though at least I can blame the grit. Not that my father or my brother seem to notice. Yasha took off as if this was a race. I want to tell him that the lower gears are best for this difficult terrain, but by rights the truck still belongs to him. It also seems natural, somehow, that Papa should be directing our departure. For once, despite the unseen dangers he has foreseen, I feel safe.

Misha is between us. He's sitting on his hands, in a tracksuit top zipped up to the throat, staring straight ahead. That look of concentration on his face reminds me of the way he watches the sky for rockets. I wish I could see things as clearly as he does, long before anyone else. Thinking back to the day my friends and I set off to find the seashore, I wonder whether we might have made it had we brought my brother with us.

'You didn't say goodbye to anyone,' I say to him now,

which briefly draws his attention. 'It may be some time before we're home.'

'I couldn't do it, Alexi. I didn't know what to say.'

'Nobody does,' I assure him, thinking how I wished I'd had more time with some of my crew. 'You just say what comes naturally.'

'I'll see them again,' he decides confidently, and peers intently through the windscreen. 'How far to Aralsk, Papa?'

'Used to be a couple of hours,' he says, and trails off, shaking his head. I reckon this track must be unrecognisable to him now, which can only heighten his fears.

I have never travelled to Aralsk myself, though I have seen the skyline from a distance a few times. There was no good reason for us to go there, after all. With the ports, resorts and harbours good for nothing now, people like us were drawn into the scrubland to scratch a living. The agents who buy our scrap like to do business out in the open, and that made sense to me. It meant any possible threat could be seen coming from miles around. Now that we are preparing to leave it all behind, I realise that this is the one landscape that I know how to use to my advantage.

We drive without speaking for some time, each of us lost in thought. After what seems like an age, we pass an elderly goat-herdsman in a tunic and fedora hat, who lifts his cane to greet us. My father steers wide to pass his rag-tag flock, as if expecting one to bolt in front of us.

'Papa,' I say, eventually. 'We're on our way now. You have nothing more to fear.'

'I just don't like it. I cannot shake the feeling, Alexi.'

'Have faith,' I say, and settle back for the ride. Just as I do so, my brother leans forward and rests both hands on the dash.

'Papa is right,' he says, under his breath.

I pay attention when Mish comes out with this kind of comment. For even if there is no evidence to back up his instincts, all too often he turns out to be right. I look around, but find nothing to concern me. Any change to the landscape is so slight I barely notice. On either side of the track, all I see are low-lying dunes capped by shrub and salt. The sky is clear and empty, with a sun so weak it takes me a second to locate it. As we travel, I spot some camels grazing in the distance and then the burnt-out wreck of an old car. It's been there some time, judging by the rust and the way the sand has blanketed one side, but it's not unusual to see this kind of thing. It's only when my father appears to slow down without reason that I ask out loud if I am missing something.

'Can't you smell it?' Yasha winds down his window all the way and inhales deeply.

I glance at my brother.

'Chemicals?' Mish suggests, which is just what I am beginning to fear.

'Papa, whatever it is you should close the window. Any kind of strong odour out here is not good a sign.'

'You're wrong,' he tells me, clearly enchanted by whatever is in the air. There's no sense of brooding in his expression any more. If Yasha was still troubled about what lay in store for us, it isn't an issue right now. 'My God, this takes me back.'

Without a word of warning he veers from the track, towards the eastern ridge that once marked the coastline. The truck bottoms out immediately, only to spring back on one side as he continues to career off-course.

'Slow down!' I shout over the engine, struggling to stay on the bench. 'Where are you going?'

'Have faith, my boys!' he yells.

Just as I think my father has lost his mind, and is about to deliver us over the ridge into oblivion, he reaches for the handbrake and pulls up hard on it. The truck slides around by ninety degrees, which sends my kid brother slamming into me. It takes us both a moment to realise that we have stopped, marked as it is by the sound of the driver's door shutting.

'Papa!' I yell, and reach for my own door handle. 'Come back!'

We find him standing at the lip of the ridge. It doesn't look safe, like the earth might give way beneath his feet, but something beyond has drawn him here. Something that has left him spellbound. The first thing I pick up on is the sound of a heavy engine labouring in the distance. Then it is my nose that tells me to be careful when I approach the edge. I step up to join my father, unwilling to alarm him, and gasp at what I find.

'When I told you that nothing more could take my breath away,' says Papa, 'I was wrong.'

The sapling trees at the foot of this ridge form a shore

like I have never seen before. Each one stands no more than a couple of feet high, supported by the kind of splint and brace that remind me of callipers for lame children. There are dozens of them, divided into a patchwork of pens by paths and chainmail fencing. A tractor is making the noise I had heard. It's towing a trailer packed with yet more trees, heading for an empty pen where a gang of workmen are hacking out trenches. We figure they have been sited behind this ridge for shelter. The endless wind may be one factor, I say, but what about the soil? The salt from the shrinking sea had already killed our farmland, which in turn drove out the wildlife. So how could anything survive? My father doesn't answer, but nor does he stop grinning, and I figure the solution must be down there somewhere.

Only Misha remains unmoved by what we have found. 'We should go,' he urges from behind us.

I turn to find he isn't even looking down at this virgin plantation. He has his back to the ridge, in fact, as if this first stab at breathing life back into the region is doomed somehow. It's the coastal track we've covered so far that concerns him. Salt and sand have begun to swirl across in places, as far as we can see. If the wind picks up any more, we can expect to see dust twisters forming. At any other time, it would be fun to chase one down. Right now, I sense the back of my neck begin to prickle. I tell myself it's just grit in the air, but when my brother returns to the cab I join him without word. I am anxious to keep moving, as is Mish. Before I call for my father, I leave him alone for a minute. When he does turn, he seems changed somehow. He stands tall, looking younger than his years, and beams at us through the windscreen.

The discovery changes the mood in our cab. My father won't stop talking, mostly about how this dead and empty land is just a blank canvas in the right hands, while Misha retreats further into silence. I even jab my brother in the ribs at one point, just to check he's still with us. He doesn't respond as I had hoped, with a wriggle or a curse. He simply frowns and tightens his gaze, which is more than enough for me. Knowing that he's just concentrating, I find it's best to leave him alone. Whether or not he really does have a sixth sense, his eyes and ears are undoubtedly sharper than mine. Even Papa appears to have rediscovered his wits, it seems, when the truck approaches a gentle shelf onto an old flood plain. Just as the expanse beyond opens up, mottled brown by gorse, he glances across at us and says: 'Do you see the port, boys? There's no going back now!'

In the second or so before the truck reaches the plain, I can just make out a charcoal trace on the horizon that might perhaps be buildings and cranes. All points seem to lead there, as if every ridge of sand fans from its heart.

'We've a long way to go before we get there,' mutters Misha. A moment later, he points across me at what looks like a faraway fin of dust cutting in across the plain. I have to squint before I spot the motorbike. It seems to be heading for the same place as us. I am intrigued for a second, but that's quickly overtaken by alarm when my father spots another one coming in.

'We have company!' he yells, his attention split between the dust track and his side window. Even before I see the second bike I am seized by dread. For it's clear we're caught in some kind of pincer movement. Instinctively, I realise there is only one way to escape such an execution, and that's to turn and flee. One glance in my side-mirror confirms my worst fears.

There it is in our wake: a dune buggy rattling through the dust.

I have never seen The Bat in daylight. If he has defied the darkness to hunt us down then it is clear he means business. The buggy has only just dropped onto the plain but it's gaining ground, and fast.

'Ambush!' Misha slams the dashboard with his little fist. 'Why won't these devils leave us alone?'

'This land breeds savages!' my father yells over the engine noise. 'And savages don't give up until there's blood on their hands!'

I think of the money folded away in my back pocket. The spoils we made from laying claim to the booster rocket. I consider just flinging all the cash out of the window, let the Horde chase every dollar bill in the wind, but then this is our rail ticket out of here, as well as food and lodging for our stay in the old capital. We have left without arranging travel papers, but I know how to get money talking. All I need is a chance to make it happen. It's a chance that slims by the second, I fear, as both bikes close in on us. We're near enough now for me to see that each one carries a passenger. Then I see the one on my side point a gun in our direction.

'Get down!' I yell at my father and my brother, who looks at me like I am joking. 'This is *not* child's play!'

We all hear the bullet strike the side panelling. Then a second volley strafes the driver's side, further back down the truck. I expect Papa to freak out completely. Instead he whoops and hunches over the wheel.

'Hold on tight!' He sounds almost gleeful, as if he's waited all these years for a moment like this to come alive.

'You'll never make it!' I shout across at him. 'Papa, don't be mad at me, but I keep a pistol under the driver's seat.'

'The company you keep,' he yells over the engine roar, 'I'm relieved!'

'I can get it.' Misha reaches down for the gun, comes back with it in both hands like he's discovered some holy relic. 'Make it count, brother.'

I glance in the side-mirror once again, the truck shaking violently at this speed. The buggy on our tail is so close now that I can see Baatarsaikhan behind the wheel. That storm trooper's helmet is unmistakeable, but it's the sub-machine gun he brandishes with one hand that seizes my attention. I recognise the model by the curved magazine rack and wooden stock. It's a Soviet kalashnikov: one of the lightest assault weapons you can pick up on the black market, and the most lethal. Before my own paltry sidearm reaches my hand, I see fire spit from the muzzle of his gun, as reflected in the mirror, and then my take on him explodes with the glass. Every shard twists and tumbles from the frame. Suddenly, there is nothing left of it but a torn-up plastic stump, and all I can think is that I'm facing the last moments of a journey that has hardly begun.

12

I can't take my eyes from the splintered stump, shocked senseless by what is unfolding here. I try to focus, to think ahead. We're still hurtling across what passes for a track, bidding for the closing space between the two bikes, but all I can do is watch helplessly. I hear my brother and my father yelling over one another and the mounting roar from the bikes. With nothing to lose, I wind down the window and use my gun sight to find the buggy right behind us. My eyes start streaming immediately and I have to squint to find what I'm looking for. I curl my finger around the trigger, wishing I had Lena's cool, confident control. The truck shakes and shudders, my bead on Baatarsaikhan bouncing sharply, but I know I have to make this shot count. I find that storm trooper helmet in my sights, steady my aim until I am sure Baatarsaikhan has seen me. I see him draw his own weapon, but the track here is thick with shingle. From experience, I know it demands a sure grip on the wheel, which means there's no way he can lock onto me with only one free hand.

Suddenly, The Bat has become a sitting target, and I sense that he knows it. I think of what I'm about to do, see him roar something at me. A defiant final cry, I think, inviting me to bring it on. I tighten my trigger finger, zoned in now on nothing else but him.

And finally, just before firing, I lift the gun skywards.

'What was *that*?' Misha drags me back onto the bench. He is in my face immediately, bringing with him all the noise and dust and drama that I had just tuned out. 'You could've taken him down, Alexi! Why are you wasting bullets?'

I am in shock. I recognise this in myself. But I also feel quite calm and certain of my actions. I refuse to give my rival money or blood, but I will give him respect. I owe him that, at the very least.

'It was the right thing to do,' I shout across the bench, aware that the next move is out of our hands.

Misha has no time to question me, for another crack rings out on the driver's side, and a bullet sings through the quarter light. Both machines are racing level with the cab now, with the outriders preparing to board us. There's no stopping my father, however. The truck is moving faster than ever before, but still it's not enough, I shout across. *We'll never beat these bikes!*

'We're outgunned and we're outnumbered,' Papa calls back. 'But let's find out if we've also been outwitted.'

I see what he is about to do just before he wrenches the wheel sharply to one side. All I can do is grab Misha and brace us both as the truck slams into the first riders and then switches back for the others. I hear startled cries, stuttering engines and the sound of metal tumbling over sand. When I dare to look out, both bikes have simply vanished. I glance back and catch my breath at the sight of all four of them in the dust. My heart turns to ice when I think that we have killed people here, but they all come alive as the dune buggy bears down on them. The Bat fishtails to avoid one rider, only to barrel into the wreckage of a bike. The impact stops the buggy dead. Even before the maddened roar of the engine falls idle, I see my rival throw off his harness to square up to his fallen soldiers.

'We did it!' Misha sounds like he has been holding his breath since Papa made his move. He twists from my embrace with both fists raised, while Yasha refreshes his grip on the wheel, looking quietly pleased with himself.

'We all did it,' he says, glancing over my brother at me.

I nod at him without smiling, wishing he had not been lost for us all this time, and then turn my attention to the way ahead.

Pylons, oil pipes and scrap that can't be salvaged mark the outskirts of Aralsk. We pass great cable spindles and half-submerged shipping containers. Some have doors peeled back like empty food tins, with driftwood piled high inside. Flaking paintwork clings to some of the timber lengths, which makes me wonder out loud whether we're looking at boat remains.

'Maybe so,' says Papa. 'A ship isn't much use without a sea, after all. Better to break it up for firewood than to let it rot and decay.'

I say nothing in reply, struck as I am by this upswing in his outlook. Our skirmish with the Horde had left me reeling. It also proved that Yasha was not lost to us, and now here he was sounding positive for once. Mish had celebrated outrunning them for a short while after, but I was relieved when he settled. I didn't like seeing him too anxious or over-excited. During the last few months it had often triggered minor seizures, and I don't think any of us could cope with that right now. I just feel very tired – overwhelmed by the events of recent days and the upheaval we now face. We are leaving home, after all. I had been waiting for this moment for a long time, but never thought I'd be so rattled and unprepared. Only my father's mood continues to brighten, most strikingly on the subject of his long-lost sea. I see little reason to be so cheery, especially as this former port looms large. Wharves, cranes and forgotten gantries break up the skyline, while the stranded ships on the seaward side are bigger than any I have seen before. Even the wind seems more ferocious than it does back home, hurling great breakers of sand over what must have been the promenade. We begin to pass other vehicles on the outer roads, also children selling fuel from jerry cans. My father nods at some of the kids, though none respond in kind, and as we leave the seabed behind, so his chatter trails away.

We drive in silence through the run-down blocks and boulevards behind the port. Having travelled for miles across an empty expanse, all three of us peer up and around. It looks like any other half-abandoned outpost. Just a little bigger than most. Across walls and rooftops, there are hoardings that have been bleached in the sun and salt. It's as if the advertisements for tobacco and motor oil have given up the ghost, and no longer see the point in trying to attract attention. We pass young men on corners, killing time as ever, and seemingly indifferent to the stinging wind. Those people on the move clutch shawls or sleeves to their mouths, and walk in the streets with the traffic. Sand and dust stream over every surface. It drops from rooftops and gathers in gutters, sweeping across roads and pavements. We drive at a crawl through this weird spray, steering round kicked-looking dogs and cockerels. There are no signposts, and yet Yasha appears to know exactly where he's heading.

'Things must have changed since you were last here,' I say finally, when the station swings into view.

My father doesn't reply straight away. Instead, he pulls up under a string of traffic lights ahead of the main steps. He sighs deeply and rests back on the bench. I wonder why we have stopped. The lights aren't working and apart from several taxis outside the station entrance, there is nothing in front of us but drifting dust.

'Seems to me now things never *stop* changing,' he says, and nods at his own conviction. It's as if he has just reached this opinion, the way he pauses for so long. 'Who knows?' he continues. 'Over time, the desert could move in some more, or great forests might spring up to shelter us and stabilise the soil. This place might feel like it's finished, boys, but things are bound to be different when you return to me.'

'But you're coming with us?' Mish sounds puzzled, and then concern lifts his voice. 'We need you.'

I look across at Yasha. He dips his head, rubs his sockets with his fingertips.

'Papa?' The atmosphere thickens in the cab, but I hold out for some kind of explanation.

'This journey has shown me many things,' he says, eventually.

'Like the fact that we could all be killed if we ever cross the Molotov Horde again!' I draw breath to spell out the danger in more detail, but all he does is shrug. Stunned, I go over what he has just said. It's his talk of trees that seemed to come out of nowhere, and then it dawns on me what has caused his change of heart. 'Papa,' I start again, struggling not to sound so frustrated, 'the plantation we saw. It's an experiment, just like it was when the sea lost the rivers to the fields. You know, this place wouldn't be so cooked were if not for all the fallout from *atomic* tests. It's a sandpit for scientists, Papa. Nothing more.'

'Come with us,' says Mish, sounding close to tears.

Our father moves off from the lights now, looking straight ahead. I see the line of his throat lift and fall, but his gaze remains steady and true.

'You have to reconsider,' I appeal to him. 'We're in this together.'

'I'd only hold you back, Alexi. We all know that.'

'You got us through an ambush,' I say.

'That was down to you,' he replies, sounding measured despite our rising protests. 'What you did with your last shot counted for a lot. You spared a life. Baatarsaikhan was looking at a bullet between the eyes, but you let him go. It showed me that no matter what you face from here, you will always do the right thing.' He pulls up behind the cabs, but keeps the engine running. When he turns to face us, Misha whimpers and then buries his face in his chest. Yasha kisses the crown of his head, looking at me still, and I know for sure that his mind is made up. 'I belong in Aral, boys. I'm staying. The sea might well be gone for good, but life goes on. I can see that for myself now. For better or worse, I need to see how things change here.'

13

Our flight from here wasn't supposed to turn out like this. Bringing Papa with us had only recently become part of my plan, but now it seems unthinkable that it should be any other way. A grenade attack had opened Yasha's eyes to the fact that this region wasn't just in ruins but existed as a living danger. I had simply assumed he would want to get far away from it, same as us. Now, it seems, our journey this far had made him realise what he would be missing. I also read our father's decision for us to go without him as a declaration of his faith in me. I am sad that he is gone now, but also grateful somehow. For what he leaves me with is this: a chance to make a stand that counts.

'Alexi, I'm scared.'

'We'll be fine. The train should be here soon.'

Yasha had left us at the station steps and driven off without looking back. Misha and I had watched the truck fade into the dust, and then dodged our way onto the platform. It wasn't hard, with so few station staff and plenty of people lining up to leave this place behind. The building we had to pass through was little more than an empty shell with a ticket booth and a harassed-looking official behind it. On the wall opposite hung a huge mural showing joyful fishermen at work, as if they were blessed to have such a purpose in life. It looked years old, like a museum piece in need of restoration.

'Will we see Papa again?' my little brother asks.

I say, of course, in no time; and just hope that Denis and the crew will take care of him in our absence. We're standing some way down from the station buildings, where we won't attract attention. There are a lot of tracks here, from a time when trade was fruitful. They are divided by narrow, foot-high platforms that serve to channel the sand right now. In the marshalling yard further down from us, I see a couple of engineers pacing alongside a locomotive and her rolling stock. It's a freight train, by the look of things, with a caravan of beaten-up boxcars and petroleum cylinders. Further down the tracks, under the power lines there, I see a passenger train. It's just come to a standstill, but looks poised to swoop in and collect us at any moment. As most people are gathered on the same side as us, I reckon it won't be long before we leave our troubles behind.

'Promise me something,' I say to Mish next. 'If you so much as get a bad feeling along the way, any kind of weird sense like you do when something is about to fall out of the sky, I want you to tell me right away.'

'Why? What is there to worry about now?'

'Just swear to me you'll speak up, let me fret about what it might be.'

'I can do that,' he agrees, like it's no big deal. 'If it makes you feel better.'

100

We could expect to be spot-checked on the way by the transport police, and I figured this might cause problems. You can't move around in this country without paperwork to prove who you are, but we'd had no time to get all of ours in order. Sometimes it seemed like the authorities made travel tough to stop people breaking out and reminding the world of our existence. I didn't care what damage had been done to the region any more. I just wanted my brother to get well again. I figured kids like us wouldn't get into trouble if we failed to dodge an inspection on the train. We simply looked like lost boys, and I would spin them a story around that, or show them some money to buy a blind eye. Most probably, we would be ordered off at the nearest station. It might hold us up for a while, but only until the next train arrived. At the very worst, we might face an escort home. Even then, we would simply turn around and try again. Giving up just wasn't something I have ever done before. No matter how futile things could become, a son of Aral would find a way to get through it.

'How are you feeling now?' I ask Misha, thinking of what we have faced just to get this far. He lifts his shoulders for a moment, kicks idly at the belted roll of belongings in front of him. 'We'll soon be on our way,' I tell him. 'In a couple of days, we'll arrive at Almaty. If you like, we could take a look around before we head for the hospital. We could use some time to rest, I think. It's about time we enjoyed ourselves.'

'Where will you stay?' He looks up now, finds me smiling broadly.

'Right beside you,' I assure him. 'I'm your brother, aren't I?'

'If I were you,' Mish says next, as a grin breaks out across his face. 'I'd try to be more like me.'

I clip the back of his head, laughing with him at such nonsense. 'Why would I want to be the runt, huh?'

'This runt packed for the journey,' he says, prodding at the roll once more with his foot. 'Without me, Alexi, you'd have nothing.'

'So what have we got?' I drop my roll from my shoulder and loosen the belt strap to look inside.

'The blanket and a few spare clothes in each.'

'Is that it?'

Papa didn't give me much time.'

I stop short of unrolling it, and frown at him instead. 'What are we going to do for food and drink on the journey? And what am *I* going to do for cigarettes? It's two days to the old capital, little Mish.'

'We'll manage,' he says. 'Won't we?'

I glance along the platform, watching out for anyone faintly official. 'We always do,' I say with a sigh. 'Though maybe the first thing we should visit on arrival is some place to *eat*.'

I feel better as the minutes pass, just horsing around together. It reminds me how things were before he got sick. A long time has passed since we enjoyed a moment like this: poking fun at each other to forget about ourselves. All the while, I think about our father, and I sense it is the same for Mish. I picture old Yasha behind the wheel, travelling back to where he belongs, but with his eyes wide open this time. I don't want to think about what he might find, though if my father is to be believed then he is ready for anything. I hope I can say that we're equally prepared, and look back anxiously at the waiting train. There it is, way down the line, still holding for the signal. Dust and sand drift over the rails in front of it, while a glint of light on glass draws my attention across to the marshalling yard. The locomotive is beginning to pull out, I see. Behind it, the freight wagons clank and complain as if seeking some kind of order. Mish and I have witnessed trains from a distance, slipping across the steppes, but this is the first time we have faced one head on. I call for my brother to watch, pleased that the train is about to clear the way for our own. It's only when he fails to answer that I glance over my shoulder and find him looking in the opposite direction.

'What is it?' I ask, coming around now. His face is completely frozen, his eyes wide and unblinking.

'You wanted me to tell you when I got a bad feeling,' he whispers.

I search the platform, see nothing unusual. Just as I am about to press him for an explanation, those people in front of the station buildings suddenly turn and move apart, as if some kind of animal has just broken loose. Instinctively, I reach for the pistol I have tucked behind my belt, and then freeze at what I see. My sights lock onto the figure coming through with the sub-machine gun. A second later, I register the fact that he's glowering directly at us. Baatarsaikhan advances slowly, his weapon tipped back so the muzzle rests upon his shoulder. I think about what might happen if I attempt to draw my own measly pistol, which persuades me to leave it where it is.

'I thought I should come to see you off,' he calls to us, seemingly unconcerned by the risk he is running. 'I'm sorry I'm late,' he adds. 'Engine trouble.'

I appeal to someone for help, but already the people behind him are hurrying from the platform. The few that remain simply stand and stare helplessly, just like little Mish.

'Take the money.' I grab the banded wedge of notes I have stashed in my pocket and hurl it into the dust. 'It won't stop us leaving.'

The Bat chuckles, closing in on us now, and steps right over it.

'This isn't just about money any more, Alexi.'

I tell my brother to pick up his blanket as I have, and begin to back away.

'I know what it's about. Only the strongest survive, right?'

'It's the rules,' he says, like it can't be helped. 'Is there a problem?' He tips his head to one side, clearly playing with us.

Behind us, a blast from the locomotive's air-horn tells me I have no time to spare. I grab Mish by the wrist and rush for the tracks.

'Alexi, no!'

I register my brother's protest but there's no time to change my mind. As soon as I leave the platform I sense that the train is much closer than I had judged. I can feel a wall of air pushing towards me, but I don't look round. Nor do I let go of his hand, even when he stumbles in the ballast bed and falls to one knee. Instead, I reach around with my other hand and haul him clear by the wrist. The big wheels slice by just behind him, the horn sounding once again – in anger, it seems to me. My brother scrambles to his feet, his jeans sooty at the knee, but follows me without question. I just want to get us out of range, using the train as cover, but as I race alongside now I realise it won't last long. The locomotive is beginning to move a fraction faster than us, gathering pace all the time, and I feel some panic rising as the first boxcar glides by. The sliding door to this one is shut, while I can't quite reach the ladder at the back. There's no time now to draw my gun. Nor is there any point, it seems, in view of what we're fleeing from here. If The Bat finds us in his sights, we would be cut down by a storm of lead. The door to the next boxcar is open, with a chain swinging loose from one handle. I try to grab it, but a rattle of gunfire makes me duck on instinct, and my hand closes round thin air. The Bat has followed us across the rails after the final wagon. I glance back and see him standing there. He has the gunstock pressed to his hip this time, aiming directly at me.

'We only have one more chance,' I shout breathlessly at Misha. This time, I am not prepared to mess up. As the next boxcar passes, I throw my roll through the open door and then reach out for my brother's hand. As soon as our fingers mesh, I swing with all my might. Little Mish slams against the edge of the wagon. His legs swing under for a second, but then he lifts and scrambles inside with a triumphant yell.

'You can make it too, Alexi!' He's there at the door, kneeling at the edge now, with his hand outstretched, but already the gap between us is widening. The next round of gunshot causes the ballast just behind my heels to spread in all directions. My heart is hammering, both legs losing strength, and all I can do is urge little Mish to save himself. I watch his face melting as the boxcar clears me entirely, and cry out in defeat and desperation. I come to a halt, rest my hands on my knees for a beat, and then turn as if facing my maker.

'Do it, then!' I scream at him. 'Come and finish this!'

I spread my palms, my chest heaving hard, but the shot doesn't come. I look up slowly, see The Bat still braced to take me out. The last wagon has cleared me now, revealing a deserted platform.

'Say goodbye,' he says. 'We're done now.'

I squeeze my eyes shut. I'm trapped here, with no option now but to take the hit in my brother's name.

'Come *on*!' I scream at him, 'Just let Misha go.'

I draw breath, sense only silence in the wind. It's then I realise that I can no longer hear the locomotive, just the distant sound of my brother pleading. I open my eyes, face The Bat once more. He's still poised to shoot, only now he nods at something behind me. I glance around, see the train down the line, stationary under a red signal light. I gasp, turn back, and realise he has been waiting for this moment. Without word, he lifts the sub-machine gun high and fires off a volley into the sky.

I don't move a muscle, blink or breathe. I just meet his gaze midway, sure that he can sense my respect.

'*Alexi, it's moving off!*'

I hear my brother's appeal, the wheels grinding into motion once again. Coolly, The Bat slings the gun over his shoulder, and then touches his temple in salute.

'You're going straight to hell,' he calls out. 'Wherever you end up.'

I laugh, in sheer relief, then turn and bowl after my brother. Seconds later I catch his hand, as he had caught mine, and throw myself onto the wagon floor. He looks shocked, exhausted and elated, and weeps when I hug him close.

'We did it!' I crow, and look around. The boxcar is empty but for a few cargo crates stacked haphazardly at the front like children's building blocks. Whatever our destination, I think to myself, it has to be better than the nightmare we've just escaped. We may have lost all our money, but we're alive. For that, I have my rival to thank on both counts.

I turn to the open door, look back one final time. 'I'll see you again, my friend,' I promise, but we're too far away for him to hear. I keep watching until The Bat and then the station disappear from view. Behind the port, the sky over the seabed climbs higher as we pick up speed. On each side, the buildings and the billboards start to blur.

'We're out of here,' I say to myself, as if that might help our escape to sink in. I breathe out long and hard. Right now, I really don't care where it might take us. We'll find our way. We always do. 'Do you hear?' I turn to celebrate with my brother, discover him right behind me with a strange look on his face. 'Mish?'

'I'm sorry,' he says under his breath, which mystifies me. Then his eyes lift back into their sockets and he crashes to the floor.

'Brother, *no*!'

I drop to my knees, whispering his name over and over again as the body in front of me begins to shudder and shake. It's like every muscle in his body is possessed, threatening to tear him apart. His head snaps one way then the other, spittle and snot flying in all directions.

'I'm here,' I breathe, just in case he is aware of what is happening. 'Don't leave me now.'

I know that I am simply supposed to keep vigil, make sure he comes to no harm, but I have to *do* something this time. For it just goes on and on. I smell urine and then shit, hear him grunting and grinding his teeth. I try to cradle him, but little Mish has the strength of ten men. An elbow snaps up at me, splitting my lip wide open. I bury my face into my hands for a moment, tasting blood and tears. All the time this train thunders onward, heading out of this forgotten space and into the unknown. I just hope and pray that someone can still hear me when I throw my head back and howl.

The Kazakh Steppes, Sol-lletsk/Yaisan border. Later:

There are no shadows here at the end of the day. This vast expanse of grassland is uninterrupted, home to nothing but a lowing wind. Light settles in blankets where the sun has left the sky, and slowly powers down. But just as darkness seems inevitable, the stars emerge in force. With a grand moon rising, it could be another world this train now thunders across.

The locomotive hauls no passenger carriages, but a long chain of cargo containers. Its destination is a mystery to one stowaway on board. He's there inside a wood-panelled boxcar, kneeling beside his younger brother. Alexi Titov has never ventured so far from home in his life, but he has only one concern at this time. Two thin, woollen throws cover the nine-year-old. His face is pale, the lips lacking colour, even in this nocturnal light. It's been some hours now since the little boy's seizure, the worst Alexi has witnessed, and his eyes remain closed and quite still. Since making his brother as clean and comfortable as he can, Alexi has barely moved himself. Now, the drop in temperature and the powerful slipstream through the wagon are beginning to bite.

Alexi climbs to his feet, hugging himself for warmth, and

then tests the sliding door. It is pinned back from the outside by bolts he cannot reach, and so he turns his attention to the crates at the front of the wagon. Wherever this train is heading, he knows that at some stage it must stop and an inspection will be made. The crates look as if they're lashed into the gloom, the way the moonshine cuts across the floor in front of them. One or two at the base would certainly be big enough to climb inside and hide away, but they're stapled shut and too strong to break into. Up close there's a strong smell of animal pelts, untreated fur, most probably, which makes it all the more frustrating.

Alexi stalks around this jumble of shapes, as if seeking a way to crack a puzzle. Out on the tracks, sparks fly from the wheels. The interior jars with light and silhouette, just as he dips down to explore the gap behind the crates. Discovering what appears to be a wad of plastic sheeting, Alexi reaches in to pull a corner free. Then something back there startles him so profoundly that he snaps out his gun and braces to fire it with both hands.

14

'Don't shoot, *please*!'

I only just hear the voice over the clatter of the couplings and wheels. There is something alien to it, as well as genuine terror. Then, through the gloom, I see two palms lifting. At first I believed I had disturbed an animal, like a wildcat or a fox, but I have no idea how to handle something like this. The sheeting crackles and shifts behind the crates. I tighten my grip on the gun.

'Show yourself!' I demand, trying hard not to sound shaken. I step back several paces, and keep a bead on the dark shape that emerges from the gap. 'Who are you?'

Cautiously, this figure cuts into the slanting bars of moonlight: a girl, I realise, and about my age. What shocks me most of all is the state she is in. Her clothes make me think she has been dragged through a thorn briar and dumped in the dirt. I ask myself if the Horde might have sent her, for she shares the same eastern features as Baatarsaikhan. Beyond the shape of her eyes, however, the look in them tells me she has travelled so much further than their homeland of Mongolia. There is exhaustion in her gaze, as well as dread and fear, which makes me feel bad for keeping the gun on her. She just stands before me with her hands held high, trembling now, but not just from the cold. I ask her name, offering mine straight away in the hope that it might help.

'*Tao.*' She sounds as if she's been holding her breath. It comes out in a rush, like it took some courage to find her voice. 'Don't shoot.'

'Why are you here, Tao? Are you spying on us?'

All I see is panic tighten into her expression. 'Don't shoot,' she pleads yet again. It's as if she has only one phrase to deal with this situation. Like something she's been forced to say, perhaps, many times before.

'Where are you from?' I speak slowly, calmly, my voice only raised so she can hear me over the train. She nods when I repeat myself, and I sense she understands.

'A bad place,' she whispers finally, picking out each word. Whether it is all she is prepared to reveal, or her best effort with language that is not her own, I know exactly what she means. More sparks fly from under the boxcar just then, lighting up this strange, oriental angel from a different angle now. Her eyes drop to the floor, where Misha lies so still.

'My brother,' I say. 'I need help for him.'

She nods again, interpreting my tone perhaps, and then glances at the gun one more time. I want to put it away, but I can't risk dropping my guard, especially when she brings her hands in towards her chest. Her eyes remain locked onto mine, appealing for me to trust her, before she unbuttons a tatty, pink, quilted coat. I watch her fold it carefully, and realise what she's doing just before she crouches beside my brother. I join her and help to lift his head so she can slip this makeshift pillow underneath. I think I might cry at this act of kindness, and cover my mouth with the back of my gun hand. Then it occurs to me that she must have seen everything already, from Misha's fall to the rage and the tears that followed.

'He is lucky,' she says finally, 'you are good brother.'

I smile from behind my hand, unconcerned now that my eyes are filling.

'It's been a long journey,' is all I can say in reply.

This time, it is her turn to understand exactly what I mean. She looks at me sympathetically and then at my brother. I watch her stroke his hair, and then remind myself to breathe when little Mish opens his eyes.

'Hello,' she says, so brightly it's as if she knew he would surface at this moment.

'Don't try to speak.' I find his hand and squeeze it. 'Just rest. I'll find help, wherever we end up.'

His eyes turn to find me, and then close once more with a faint smile on his lips. It's enough for me to beam at him and then at the girl called Tao. I don't care who she is all of a sudden, or why she is riding this railroad through the middle of nowhere. My kid brother is with me once again, back from the dead it seemed. Tao looks at me like I might be crazy, still cautious despite the fact that I have tucked my gun away.

'The end,' she says to me, and I can see she is frustrated because it isn't the word she wanted. 'It is . . . not safe.'

I frown at the space between us, considering what this must mean. 'Do you know where we are heading?' I ask, thinking any kind of outpost would be better for us than the one we have just got through. Tao nods, says something in a tongue I cannot fathom. I shrug, at a loss just as she is, and watch her look around for some other way to communicate. She settles on something I cannot see, behind the crates where she had been hiding. She motions towards it, and I invite her to go ahead. Somehow I feel that I can trust her, even though it goes against my instinct for survival. I know I should show her my gun first, in case she is planning some kind of surprise, but it just doesn't feel necessary. For wherever she has come from, and no matter why she is here, we are heading in the same direction.

I watch Tao crouch at the gap, hear the plastic sheeting crackle and shift. She comes back with a document in a plastic sleeve, and hands it to me without word. A strip of tape hangs across the top of it, and I realise that she's just torn some kind of transport declaration from one of the crates. I scan it quickly, and catch my breath when I find the destination details.

I look up, and then turn to it again just to be sure I have read it correctly.

'Brother,' I say, in case he can hear me. 'We're on our way to *Russia*!' Tao looks like she really wasn't expecting me to be so upbeat, but this goes beyond my hopes and dreams. It goes beyond borders too, and doesn't just stop there, according to the document in my hands. So long as we remain undiscovered, we will reach the capital of a country where our grandfather had been born. With our history in mind, I decide what we are doing here is returning to our roots. I know little about where we are bound, but I know it is a place that once had a profound influence on our region. If it is as rich and powerful as I imagine, capable of transforming fortunes, then I have high hopes that Moscow will be my brother's making.

Certainly, Tao doesn't share the same excitement when I spell out where we're heading. I figure it must be several days from here, but assure her it'll be worth it.

'Not safe,' she says again, clearly alarmed by my response, but there's no going back for us with this great city in our sights. From that moment on the beach outside the sanatorium, when I first learned about Misha's condition, I didn't once consider travelling this distance for help. My ambition went no further than the old capital. Our departure from Aral might not have gone to plan, but it meant we were hurtling across the steppes under moonlight towards the capital of the former motherland. Many decisions about our destiny must've been made from there, I think. Whether Baatarsaikhan has driven us onto this train by chance or design, it seems only right that we should turn to her now for the care my brother deserved.

We are going to Russia, I keep thinking, endlessly dwelling on how far we have come. *If only Yasha could see us now!*

Whatever reasons our fellow traveller had for hiding away on this wagon, I figured it was her business. With Misha sleeping deeply, I was simply happy for Tao's company. As the temperature continued to drop, it made sense for us to haul him across to the crates. There, we turned the plastic wrapping into a blanket all three of us

115

could huddle underneath. Tao refused her coat when I tried to return it to her, but accepted the spare sweatshirt my brother had rolled into my blanket. Then, over the next hour, she inched closer until she was right beside me. I could feel her shivering, but slowly our shared heat seemed to bring some stillness. By the time she dared to rest her head upon my shoulder, I had already closed my eyes. The wheels on the track and the headlong wind played like a rhythm to my ears. It was hard to resist, holed up like this on a night train that was going places, travelling with a sense of peace.

15

I couldn't be sure who fell asleep first. All I know is that we both snap awake to a steady squeal of brakes. I leap to my feet, as does Tao, and struggle to get my bearings in the darkness.

'Alexi, what is happening?' My kid brother stays where he is, propped up against the crates. He sounds weak and in a muddle. I hiss for him to keep quiet and creep on all-fours to the wagon door. The night is still with us, but as the train slows to a crawl we pass signalling and some corrugated buildings lit up from the inside.

'It's a checkpoint,' I whisper, wincing as the vapour from my breath slips into the light. Some voices next, up towards the front of the train, and then a sudden dog bark. With my palms still pressed to the floor, I dare to put my nose around the wagon door. The first things I can make out are cigarette embers glowing in the dark. They hover and float about, some way up the track. Slowly, as my eyes adjust, I see the figures smoking them take shape. Then I realise they are heading this way. I hear their boots crunching over the stones, and see attack dogs straining at the leash. I catch my breath, just as a hand grabs my jacket from behind and hauls me back into the wagon.

'*Not safe!*' Tao jabs a finger at the crates, and I know just what to do. The voices are clear now and closer. The sound of men issuing orders to their dogs. I hear them investigate a boxcar in front, and fear this search is going to be our undoing. My brother makes an attempt to sit up. As he does so, the sheeting we had used to cover him crackles like tinder on fire. The three of us freeze, but it's too late now. Without doubt the guards have heard it, because some excitement comes into their voices. All I can do is stare at Mish and Tao, sensing this journey might soon be over. More crunching over the ballast bed now, directly outside our wagon. I prepare to show myself, rather than risk us all being set upon, but something holds me back. A commotion from the boxcar *behind* ours. Shrieking and panic-stricken voices, I realise, spilling out onto the tracks.

Like the guards, it takes a moment for me to connect with what's happening. There are children everywhere, sprinting under moonlight as if their lives depended on it. All of them are screaming and yelling, fanning out between buildings and into the night. I hear Tao declare something in her mother tongue, sounding almost overjoyed. It's chaos outside, with dogs off the leash, several adults shouting now, then a rapid burst of gunfire. The sound decays across the plain, and that's when Tao makes a bolt for the door. She just springs up beside me, with no warning or explanation.

'What are you doing?' I grab her by the arm, shocked

to find her twist around and snarl at me. 'Are you crazy? Stay down!'

She tries to pull away once more, as if caught by a trap, but I hold on tight. More shots snap into the night, stilling us both. A man's voice cries out in surrender, sounding as furious as he does defeated. I turn, with Tao, to see a tall figure picked out by torchlight. He has thinning hair pulled back in a pigtail, and seems to be just standing there helplessly watching the last kids melt away. Then a guard rushes up behind him and he drops to his knees, as instructed, with his hands clasped over his head. I turn to Tao, see her grinning victoriously, but with tears in her eyes.

'A bad man?' I ask in a whisper, and she nods without looking at me.

'A *smuggler*,' says Mish, under his breath.

I swap glances with my brother, and just then it dawns on me what I have witnessed.

The stock inside the boxcar behind us was not the kind to have paperwork. The figure on his knees out there was a trader in *people*.

I look at Tao in a fresh light. Her reason for being on board this train makes sense to me now. But even if she was travelling against her will, and had managed to escape as far as the next wagon, I could not understand why she would want to make a break for it here. Moscow is waiting for us at the end of the line, which just had to offer more than this barren border crossing. I didn't like to think how those kids would fare, in a never-ending space with no words they might use to get them home. If we made it

119

to the city, I decided, Tao would thank me for it. Right now, despite her evident pleasure on seeing this man escorted away, she refuses to meet my eye. I want to assure her that I did the right thing by keeping her with us, but we're not out of earshot just yet. Guards continue to search the area, sweeping flashlights over the ground and talking among themselves. They sound bored, I think, as if this is something that happens on a regular basis. I see one use a stick to probe the long grass behind a hut, then give up and play-fight with his dog. It's a huge white hound with pointed ears, some kind of shepherd, I think. Certainly, the brute is big enough to drag the guard off balance when they wrestle with the stick. I shift my weight from one foot to the other, aching from my time on the floor. I make no sound, at least not to *my* ear, which is why it takes a second to register that the dog has dropped the stick because of me.

I freeze, and then flinch at the barking that follows. The guard is on it straight away, grabbing the shepherd's leash as it launches towards us. The leash snaps tight, forcing this frenzied hound onto its hind legs. Other guards join them now. I see the handler elect to release the dog, but this time I don't care if I make a sound. Nor does Tao, who shrinks into the shadows with me. She squeezes herself into the gap behind the crates where I first found her, but I can't leave Misha to face this alone. I drop down to haul him back with us, sense him stiffen as I lock my arm under his. I catch his eye now, thinking this is no time for fear to get a grip, just as a wraith-like mass springs through the doors.

120

The dog's muzzle brushes the floor, ears pricked, haunches braced. It's muscular and sleek-looking, trained for moments such as this. I hear it sniff, growl, and see the shape of its head lift towards the crates. We're in total darkness, here in this quarter of the wagon, and yet there are other senses at work that I cannot detect.

A beam of torchlight swings in behind the hound, but the guards have several yards to go before they reach the wagon. I move to shield my brother, but find resistance from him again. Without word, Misha rocks forward onto his hands, and meets the dog face on.

'What are you doing?' I hiss.

A low growl shuts me up. It sounds threatening and also curious, but Mish doesn't back down. I see my brother's eyes tighten, feeling sick with fear. The growl becomes a snarl, the dog's ears flattening now, its body dropped low. For a moment, I think it looks set to leap upon my fearless little brother. There are guards at the wagon door now, chest-high to the floor with pistols and torches. *We are finished*, I think, as a beam drops down the wall towards us.

And then the dog turns away.

I watch this beast slink back to its handler with none of the aggression with which it had arrived. The handler grasps its collar to reattach his leash, glances briefly into the gloom that hides us, and then orders the dog out of the wagon. The torch beams pull away in turn and muttered conversation accompanies the footsteps over the ballast.

Seconds later, I hear the guards encourage the dog to

jump into the next truck. I feel relief and utter amazement, read the same thing in Tao's face as she peeps out from behind the crates. The pair of us turn to my brother. He hasn't moved since the dog retreated. His eyes are closed now, but there's a faint smile there. Whether he just glared down the dog or something more, I want to tell Tao that my crew always said he was different from the rest. I know she won't understand me, but I stay quiet for a more pressing reason. For I dare not even sigh with relief until this train is safely on the move again.

16

I know we are close to our journey's end. The train has begun to slow steadily, the speed dropping like the temperature. Some time has passed since we first holed up in here. Two days, maybe three. We have gone without food or water, and the cold is beginning to pinch, but Mish and I have known worse. Back at the checkpoint, the train crew had come along and secured every wagon, under orders from the guards. I heard cross words traded, and figured losing so many stowaways across the steppes would cause trouble for one side or the other. Then the wagon door was hauled shut, confining us to darkness. As the train rolled on, all I could do was guess at our place in the world.

I didn't need to see my travelling companions to know that Tao had much on her mind, while my brother really needed a hospital bed. I knew this because of the quiet crying I would hear from her on occasion, and the fact that when Misha slept he went down dangerously deep. At one point, the smell of fresh urine cut into the cold air. I had already changed him into what clothes he had packed, the last time this happened. All I could do was hope that it would dry on him before he surfaced, sparing him embarrassment. When I peed, only once because we'd had nothing to drink, I took myself to the furthest corner. There, consumed by shame, I closed my eyes and told myself this hardship would soon be over.

I barely heard Tao move at all. After the checkpoint, she went back to the gap behind the crates where we first found her. And that's where she stayed. I just could not understand why she had turned against me after such a narrow escape. If she hadn't been captured racing from the wagon, she would've handed herself in after one night wandering the steppes. The freedom out there could overwhelm, unless it was all that you knew. I put her bid to flee down to panic, and hoped she would change her mind about me when we arrived.

It had been nice, huddled up with her. Keeping warm may have been our aim, but I also felt comforted after everything that had happened. Above all, it made me think of Lena, and what she had said as we left. Growing up in such a harsh environment, I had always looked to her for one thing: cover, as we picked over crash sites. Without her now, I began to wonder if it wasn't just her eyes and ears that I depended on, but her presence in my life. I dwelled on this for some time, long enough to know that I had to stop thinking about it.

I had left home for my brother, I reminded myself. Misha was the one who needed care and protection. Not me. And with that thought I had drawn my knees up to my chest, and waited for this journey to be over.

Inside the boxcar, shut away from the world, I begin to notice a change in the air. I feel sure we left the open country behind some time ago. The earthy smell of grass and rain is long gone, and for a while I can only imagine the kind of terrain that might be rushing by. Then, in the last hour or so, all sorts of industrial fumes have begun to creep in. I know I am hungry, which has perhaps sharpened my senses, but I feel like I am sucking on a coin. The taste won't go away, even when I spit between my feet. When the train begins to slow, I figure I'll just have to live with it.

'This *must* be Moscow,' I whisper finally, as we move from a crawl to a series of gentle lurches. All around us, fissures in the wooden panelling tell me it is at least daytime. It is also enough for me to see that my brother has opened his eyes. If he feels anything like me, the pit in his stomach must be keeping him from sleep now. Even so, I am confident that we will soon be out of here. 'Listen to me, Tao?' We won't abandon you when we arrive, I promise. We'll make sure everything is good for us all!'

Tao may speak a different language, but she pretends not to hear me. I glance at Misha. He pulls a face. I shrug like it doesn't matter, wishing at the same time that I knew more about her. Is she running away from home, or has she been forced out, even sold on, like livestock? Wherever she has come from, I just want her to know that I have high hopes about where we are going.

'Can we prise open the door?' Mish pauses to make

himself more comfortable. 'Just a little bit, so we can see the city.'

I tell him once we're sure of a clear exit, we'll find out what's in store for us. 'Use your imagination for now,' I suggest instead.

I watch him shut his eyes, concentrating hard. His faith in me makes me smile. We might've had to grow up fast in our world, but Mish would always be a little kid at heart.

We crawl for several minutes. I am aware of other trains passing on both sides, all of them at quarter speed, and figure we should make a break for it soon. For if the train was heading for a station terminal, we would only find ourselves among guards and other officials.

Finally, we come to a halt, though I suspect it is only temporary. I hear the locomotive's engine ticking over, a dripping sound between the wagons, and a steady hum all around.

'What is that?' asks Mish. This time, even Tao is looking to me, as if perhaps I can see through the walls of the wagon. I listen some more. The sound of traffic begins to take shape, coming from every direction and distance. It reminds me of a never-ending sigh. Like my mother's last breath, is what I can't help thinking. I keep it to myself, but feel a strong need to get out into the open.

I cross the wagon floor and lean into the edge of the door. Using my shoulder and, finally, a good kick, something cracks and pings away on the outside. I figure I must've broken some kind of security seal, placed there to stop further tampering, because the door now slides back and forth, but only by an inch. The gap is wide enough for me to see a locking pin. I just can't squeeze my fingers beyond the knuckles to free it. Then smaller, slender hands appear beneath my own. I glance at Tao, pleased to see her working with me, and catch my breath when she finds what I failed to reach.

After so long in near darkness, the daylight is blinding to begin with. We both shrink away, as if the cold air is coming in to claim us.

'What do you see?' asks Misha. 'Tell me!'

I look again, with Tao beside me. We're in a wide cut between buildings, with too many tracks to count and a thin frost on the ground. Freight trucks stand empty on the far side, where weeds have grown thick as rope. A locomotive engine chugs past next, heading in the same direction as us. I follow it as far as I can from our hiding place, and realise we are much closer to the end of the line than I had thought.

'I see a station mouth about a mile from here,' I report in a whisper. 'If we end up inside it, we'll be finished before we've even begun.'

I look around some more, wondering how quickly we can clear these busy tracks, and ask Misha if he's feeling strong again.

'I can stand.' He emerges, unsteadily, from the plastic sheeting.

'But can you run?' I pause as yet another train pulls across my view. 'Once we set off, there'll be no going back.'

'I know that.' My little brother takes a faltering step

across the wagon. Tao is there for him before me. One arm around his waist, lips pressed thinly together.

'Thank you,' I say.

'We get out *now*,' she replies, with such determination I doubt anyone could stop her this time.

17

These are my first footsteps on foreign soil. There is no dust here, no sand in the wind to anger the eyes. As for the cold, I am used to hunching into an icy blast. Unlike Aral, the air here is quite still. It is just as chilling, however, and with no escape from the worst of it whichever way I turn. Even so, I am thrilled to be here. I think of Yasha, Lena, Denis and the crew, and wish that we had arrived as one. Having dropped down from the boxcar, I loosen up my limbs and fill my lungs. It may not taste quite right, but I decide it has to be safer than the stuff I have been breathing all my life.

My blanket roll hits the ballast beside me next, marking an end to this private moment.

'Please help me down, Alexi.'

My brother is next off the wagon, lowered down to me by Tao. His tracksuit top rises over his stomach when I take him, exposing his rib cage. He has always been wiry like me, but somehow it doesn't seem natural on him any more. It feels like he's built to carry more meat on his bones. I know we need to eat. I am just relieved that we are in the right place if this is his sickness showing. Without proper care, people who get ill back home just seem to fade out over time. They become like the landscape in many ways: steadily disintegrating, long after it is clear that nothing more can be done. The same thing won't happen to my brother, however. We are out of the wilderness, after all. Here at last, in the heart of a city that will be his salvation.

In the distance up the tracks, I see a train pulling out from under cover of the station. A powerful hiss from our own engine makes me think we'll be moving in next, and so I urge Tao to be quick. She jumps down with ease, absorbs the impact in her knees. Brushing her palms as she stands, this strange angel of ours mutters something like a curse or a prayer and moves off first. Little Mish makes his own way across the tracks. He follows in Tao's footsteps, looking worn out but ready for this final push, and I keep close behind.

On reaching the weeds, only Tao turns around to watch the outbound train. Mish and I explore behind the sidelined trucks here, looking for a way out. The wall here is four or five times the height of the rolling stock underneath. I am beginning to feel a little trapped. Then my brother spots a service ladder of some sort, bolted into the brickwork. I smile to myself, wondering if there would ever come a time where I saw something before him.

'Let me go first,' he volunteers. 'Please, Alexi. I can do it.'

I want to tell him that he doesn't have to keep pretending to be big and strong. We are here because he is sick, after all. Despite my misgivings, I choose to stand back this time. Anything to help him get through this.

Little Mish scales the rungs without stopping. At the top he scrambles over the wall and disappears from sight. I don't breathe out until his head reappears, framed by the clear blue sky.

'It's a different world!' he cries, too loud for my liking. 'Come and see!' It's only when I join him that I realise there is little point in keeping our voices in check.

What I question is his first impression of this city.

I don't know what I am about to find on the other side. Some kind of paradise, I think drily, judging by my brother's response. I have never seen pictures of Moscow, after all, or even a map. I learned about the world outside Aral from stories, but nothing could've prepared me for this.

'Just look!' Little Mish is standing beside Tao. They're pressed back against the wall, clearly overwhelmed. The cold, iron rungs have chilled my hands, but what really hits me as I join them is the din. The hush we had heard from the wagon became a rumble as I climbed out of the cut. At the summit it turned to raw noise, and now I know why. We're on one side of a busy avenue, with little more than a strip of dirt between the wall and the traffic. A huge parade of concrete buildings faces us from the other side, spanning the avenue as far as we can see. They look like apartment blocks, with row upon row of little windows and a frontage in need of a good clean. Strikingly, the avenue is as broad as the cut behind us. Tram wires hang overhead, also banner advertisements for perfumes, airlines and chocolates. But what truly staggers me is the mass of cars and trucks and buses flowing underneath. The vehicles are bumper-to-bumper across every lane, but moving at quite a speed. They are mostly old and grimy, leaving fumes to hang in the air like slashed veils, but some are factory fresh. I even see an oil-black car that looks like it has been stretched out, and reflects our faces in the windows as it passes.

'Did you see that?' I turn to my brother, only to find his attention is still locked onto something beyond the heaving traffic. This time I find what has left him so spellbound, and wonder how I could've missed it. Directly opposite, sandwiched between two brooding old blocks, stands a modern structure that at first looks like a giant confection. It's pink and green, criss-crossed by strings of glittering lights and fronted by columns that seem too shiny to be made from real marble. Two men stand outside the lobby doors. They're heavy-set, clearly Russian, but dressed in tailcoats and turbans. They ignore the people passing on foot, but are first to open the doors for those who choose to go in. Riding high above them all is a Persian prince. He's fashioned from illuminated tubes of light, astride an Ace of Clubs instead of a magic carpet, all of which mystifies me.

'What on earth is it?' I ask, my voice raised over the traffic roar.

'A casino,' says my brother knowledgeably. 'A place where "New Russians" come to play with their money.'

I look at him questioningly.

'I heard about this kind of thing some place,' is all he offers me.

'What place?'

'Little Disney, most probably. Brother, you can learn all about these places if you sit on the swings long enough.' He looks back across the avenue. 'Trust me. It's a casino, like they have in America.'

I had expected to see old soviet buildings like those that flank this one, but nothing this flashy. It seems like something that belonged elsewhere. And yet, judging by how busy the doormen are as customers come and go, it has clearly found a place.

I only hope we could soon say the same about ourselves. Firstly, we have to reach the other side.

I count six lanes in total. A snow-coloured shape catches my eye, midway across. A dead dog, I realise when I look back at it, lying in a narrow strip between the two traffic flows. It's a husky, I think, lean and gaunt, and has suffered one awful smash. None of the drivers pays it any attention, as if it is nothing out of the ordinary, and I wonder how long it has been there. In some ways it looks quite at peace, motionless among all this madness, but for its fur blowing one way then the other. I point it out to the other two, but they've just seen it for themselves.

'Poor thing,' says Mish. 'What can we do?'

'We should find a safer place to cross,' is the only suggestion I can offer. 'Let's go.'

Tao looks increasingly restless, I realise. It's as if every passing vehicle is some predatory beast that could snatch her at any moment. Her eyes switch from one car to the next, looking out for something I can't see.

'We should get out of this cold,' I say, and blow into my hands to get the point across. 'We're in this together,

Tao. We'll help you, really. You just have to trust us.'

I set off towards what must be the station end, then stop with a sigh when I realise only one person is with me.

'Come on, Tao.' I try to sound friendly, reassuring. 'We can't stay here.' I gesture for her to follow but she shakes her head. She seems so vulnerable, standing there in her tatty coat and trainers, looking close to tears.

'I can't feel my fingertips.' My brother says this like it's something to be proud of, and then tucks his hands under his armpits. 'We'll freeze solid unless we keep moving.'

'Please,' I say, firmly now. 'We're tired and a little bit lost. We need to eat, drink and find our feet. We could be arrested, standing here. Let's go.'

She folds her arms, but not because of the temperature, it seems to me.

'We could try the other way,' Misha suggests, 'but we really should be heading into the city, not out of it. Isn't that right, Alexi?'

I agree for his benefit, though I doubt she understands. I figure she'll come if we keep walking.

What I don't expect is for her to turn right around and climb back over the wall.

'Wait! Where are you going?'

Tao ignores me until her feet find the rails. There, she looks up from under that high-cut fringe of hers, and says, with absolute certainty, '*Home.*'

I am dumbstruck, amazed that she would want to turn her back on the opportunities that must be here somewhere. When I find my voice, she has already dropped away from view. We rush back to the wall, see only the crown of her head. She climbs down the ladder with such grace and purpose that I really don't know if I should pursue her. I call out to her instead, as does little Mish, but she is already crossing for the central rails. Our train has vanished under cover of the station terminal, but another one approaches now. Casually, Tao turns to face it, and for one ghastly moment I think the worst.

'*No!*' my brother yells. 'Not that!'

Maybe she reconsiders, or perhaps we have misread her mind, but when Tao steps back out of harm's way the pair of us recoil in relief. I come back clutching my brow with one hand, feeling both responsible for her and helpless. All we can do is watch her now, and wonder where on earth she'll take things from here. In her pink coat she's easy to spot, and I see my sweatshirt peeping underneath. I figure she can keep it, though I don't suppose she'll want to remember me by it. Certainly, she doesn't even glance back as she picks her way over the sleepers. At least not at us. When she does turn, way down there, it is clear to me that she is planning on heading along the line in exactly the same way as we arrived.

Like Tao, I switch my attention to the station mouth. The trains that leave from there must travel far and wide. Despite the shock of her sudden departure, I hope it won't be long before she finds what she is looking for.

Finally, I face my little brother, lift his chin with my fingers, and tell him we too must be on our way.

'We can't leave her,' he says, his voice cracking now.

'She'll take care of herself, Mish. She was doing pretty well until we showed up, after all. My concern now is to look after you.'

'But what about you?'

I swing the blanket roll over my other shoulder. It hides my gun now and nothing more.

'I'll survive,' I tell him, and promise myself exactly that.

18

One time when I was very little, I got lost in the dunes. I didn't wander far. My mother only had to cross the dirt road in front of our block and call my name for me to come running. Even so, for those few minutes, my surroundings became strange and threatening. A schooner on the sands had looked to me like it harboured a band of thieves and cut-throats. It had been there all my life, rusting quietly over time, but just then those dark and smashed portholes convinced me it was no longer a place to play inside. I remember hearing whispers in the wind as I turned in circles and tried not to cry, before racing towards the urgent sound of my mother's voice.

Many years later, as my brother and I pick our way now through the litter beside this thundering avenue, that same dread creeps over me. So far away from home, hemmed between a blackened wall and a torrent of Moscow traffic, everything feels like it might be conspiring against us. And the more I look around, the more I think about what we have left behind.

'We are Kazakhs,' I remind my brother, hoping to lift our spirits. 'We should be astronauts, remember? We know how to survive in a hostile world.'

'I'm not frightened,' he calls back to me. 'But I am cold, Alexi.'

'Keep to the wall,' I warn as the tailwind from yet another passing lorry hits us hard. 'Better to be cold than killed!'

There is a pavement on the other side of the avenue, but it is only wide enough for perhaps two or three people. Motor vehicles rule out here. That much is clear to me. I catch sight of some of the drivers, sealed off in their metal boxes from the fumes and this bitter chill. We have been walking for a while now, following the cut to our right, but the avenue seems endless. Once we find the station, I am sure we'll get our bearings. For now, as I keep saying to my kid brother, we must tread carefully.

'You could try asking for directions,' he suggests. 'Just be sure to speak slowly and clearly, Alexi. We speak the same language but our accents are very different.'

'I'll trust my instincts for now,' I tell him, but smile privately at his advice. 'So what else did the kids from Little Disney tell you about this place?'

'All sorts,' he states, matter-of-factly. 'The temperature can drop to minus thirty in winter.'

'We'll be long gone before the worst of the season,' I assure him, wishing at the same time that we had been better prepared for the start of it. 'And that's quite enough facts for now.'

My brother stays silent for a minute, picking his way along the edge, where I can see him. With every step, I wonder if I have done the right thing. We are in the heart of our grandfather's country, but this capital city doesn't seem as welcoming as I had imagined. Coming from Aral, I had figured by comparison it would be like some kind of paradise. I can't decide what fuels my misgivings most: the ferocity of the traffic or the cold. Without a breath of wind, the fumes are choking here, while the chill continues to tighten its grip.

'We need one of those,' is the next thing Misha says, drawing my attention to a street trader on the far side. He is standing beside a blanket with hats and scarves laid out in rows. His own scarf is arranged to cover his mouth and nose. It makes him look like a bandit, wrapped around his face like that, but I admire his resourcefulness. I catch his eye through the traffic. He looks at me hopefully, probably wondering what two kids are doing in this weather without thick coats and mittens, at the very least. Even if we had some money, there is nothing I can do. If we stepped out now we would be mown down immediately. I shove my hands inside my trouser pockets, and march onwards. To my right, over the wall, I hear trains coming and going, and figure the station entrance can't be too far away. We'd find our bearings there, I think to myself. A map maybe or some basic directions.

What I hadn't expected was to find myself in a city on this scale. I just feel so small in such a wide-open avenue, but it doesn't end there. Huge housing blocks line up beyond the cut. They appear to fan out in ranks, like soldiers at inspection. In the middle of it all I see what must be a power plant. It is really just a windowless slab with tall chimneys. A heavy kind of steam tumbles from the funnels, which makes it look brooding and monstrous.

All the time I look back at the traffic here, waiting for a break so we can run for it. Waiting in vain, it seems.

'Alexi! Up ahead!'

My brother points at something and turns to me excitedly. I scan the buildings on the other side, some with shop fronts at ground level, and give up when I have to squint.

'What is it?' I ask. 'You always could see things before anyone else.'

'This way,' he says, and picks up the pace.

I follow close behind, tell him to slow down, to conserve what little energy we have left, but little Mish ignores me. I look again along the avenue, see nothing of note but another showy casino front. And then a break between two buildings. A junction, I think to myself. A wagon is waiting to pull out there, wipers working to skim the frost clear. I can see it is an ambulance before the siren on the rooftop starts to spin. I break into a sprint, passing my brother just to be sure I am not mistaken. For what I took to be a junction is in fact a forecourt. And behind it, set back from the avenue, is a huge hospital. *This is why we are here*, I think to myself. *We have made it, at last*!

More ambulances are queuing under the entrance canopy I see, on drawing level, where a porter waits to meet the next one.

'Hey!' I call across. My face feels hot from this sudden sprint. A relief, having been caught out by this freeze. 'Over here!'

I wave madly, switching both hands over my head, but the avenue is just too wide and flayed by traffic. The

140

porter I have spotted takes collection of a gurney from the ambulance and wheels it through the crash doors. I figure someone else will be out in no time, and turn to reassure little Mish.

Only my kid brother is no longer behind me.

A wall of air slams into me from yet another passing truck, but I am rooted to the spot.

'Mish? *Misha!*'

'Here I am.'

The faintest trace of a voice.

I spin around, find him slumped against the wall behind me. His skin is pale and waxy, his lips turned powder-blue.

'Oh no.' I drop down beside him, too afraid to shake or hug him. The corners of his nose and mouth are flecked with black from such thick exhaust. He looks confused, I think, but struggling to stay with me. 'What happened?'

'Nothing.' Either Mish has suffered a minor moment, I think to myself, or he's about to be dragged into another. 'Maybe I just need to eat,' he adds, as if he knows what I am thinking. 'Just a drink would help. A drink and a lie down.'

'We can't stay here,' I tell him.

'Give me a moment, Alexi.' He closes his eyes, and then opens them smartly when I shake him.

'Please, Mish. We're so close.'

'I'm feeling better already,' he tells me, nodding to reassure himself, it seems. 'And you know what? I don't feel cold any more.'

'You keep watching me, OK? I'm not going to leave you like this.' I meet his eyes, and wait for him to nod. Then I climb to my feet and turn to face the hospital. I see another ambulance attempting to ease into the traffic, and know just what I have to do.

The first car steers around me, the driver leaning on the horn, but the cab behind is forced to brake. I glimpse a furious face, but push on across the lanes. I clear the next one, but jump back from the coach that roars across my path, and then recoil again when the next car heads right for me. At the same time, a fender clips my blanket roll, snatching it from me. I think of my gun inside, see the roll sucked under wheels, and then it is gone.

I am numb to the danger I have created for myself, with nothing but my breathing and my heartbeat in my ears. The car horns don't connect with me, and mercifully nor do the fenders I strive to dodge. And yet with every second out there I am forced into retreat. Finally, I find myself sprawled back on my elbows in the dirt, trying hard not to let my shock and frustration spill into tears.

'I'm sorry,' I say, and this time it is my brother who places his hands on me. I feel my chest heave when he rests his small head there, and when I try to apologise once more, the words catch in my throat. 'I really didn't think it would end up like this, but I just can't do it, Misha. I've made a mess of everything. We're finished.'

'Alexi, it isn't over. We're nearly there, brother.' He sits up again, looking pained in the head, and jabs his thumb over his shoulder. 'We can *see* where we need to be, can't we?'

I wipe my eyes, lock onto the hospital despite the blur of traffic. 'At least back home I knew how to take care of you,' I say. 'It didn't matter what we came up against, I always got us through it. But out here? Nothing makes sense. It's all so new. So brutal. So *wild*!'

'It's a city,' says little Mish. 'It's just a different kind of wild from the one we know, but we can survive. We always do, is what you keep telling me. It's in our blood, from birth. All we have to do now is adapt.'

'Maybe Tao made the smart move.' I push into the dirt with my heel now, unconcerned by the cars rushing just in front of us. 'Perhaps there's only one direction we should be heading.'

Mish rises to his feet, using my shoulder to steady himself. 'You're always asking me to trust you,' he says. 'Maybe it's my turn now.'

'Misha, no!' I spring forward, too late to grab my crazy brother as he steps out into the traffic. The first car swerves, as it had for me, but he keeps his composure somehow. Doesn't switch back as I had, and instead clears two then three lanes without stopping. 'Damn it all,' I mutter under all the car horns. 'You might be special to us, but nobody walks on water!'

I plunge after him, showing my palm to the oncoming traffic, mouthing apologies as I attempt to catch up. He passes the midway point now, moving slowly but surely. The traffic beyond him is thundering in the opposite direction, but he doesn't stop looking straight ahead.

This is not an instinct for survival, I think to myself. *It's a deathwish.* A car veers sharply towards me, coming out of nowhere, it seems. I stagger back by a step, cry out when something solid clips my hip. It's a wing-mirror, which springs away on impact, but sends me spinning over the bonnet of the next braking car. I'm on my hands and knees now, the flesh on my palms scraped raw, and scramble to clear the tram lane.

Once again, I find myself on the ground, broken in a different way this time, and with my brother looming over me. A grin, of all things, breaks across his face. For a beat he looks like his old self. Just some kid on a high from causing such havoc.

'So you do trust me now?' He offers his hand. I accept it, despite the stinging pain, and then the hug he wraps around my waist. 'We made it, Alexi! We crossed to the other side!'

I lean on him for a moment, still reeling from what we've put ourselves through here, and then turn to face the hospital.

'It's why we're here.' I feel beaten, bruised and raw, but none of that matters now. 'Let's get out of the cold.'

19

The security guard waits for me to finish protesting, and repeats what he has just said. 'This is a private hospital. Now, will you please clear the lobby!'

We are standing just inside the crash doors, where the guard had stopped us. Behind him, reception staff watch us from a high counter. The floor is polished marble, with tall vases beside the elevator doors. It smells of antiseptic, and the warm air is making my nose stream.

'I need help for my brother,' I say, shocked to have been stopped at all. I am forced to wipe my nose on my sleeve. The guard's disgust is evident. I just wish he'd pay Mish the same attention as me. 'He's really very sick,' I add. 'You have to let us in.'

'Get out of here,' he says gruffly, and squares up even closer.

'What's going on?' A voice from the rear of the lobby now. We turn to see a doctor step out of the elevator. He's clutching a bottle of mineral water, and is wearing a stethoscope like a tie.

'We're from Aral,' I say, as if that will explain everything.

The doctor looks me up and down. I notice salt-white

streaks running through his hair, which he sweeps back now with one hand. He has a gentle, relaxed expression, but looks like he is at the end of a long shift. He takes a sip of water, says: 'What happened to your hands?'

I hide them behind my back, embarrassed by the attention. 'My brother here is nine years old. We think he has a brain tumour. He has "moments" ', I say in one breath, 'seizures of some kind.'

'You *think* he has a brain tumour?'

'We don't have the facilities back home to be sure.'

The guard mutters something to the doctor that I don't understand. Our accents really are very different, just as Mish had warned, and they speak much faster than we do.

'And you're here without papers,' he says, to check. 'No passports or ID cards?'

'Please!' I say, almost cutting him short. 'We're desperate.'

The doctor seems to read us for a moment, then screws the cap back on the bottle and presses it to my chest. 'Take this,' he says. 'It's all I can offer.'

'Water?' I am stunned. In Aral, water is at the heart of our crisis. Even if he meant well by the gesture, I feel insulted. 'We didn't come here for this!'

'It's a miracle that you've come here at all,' the doctor replies, and I can see he is shocked at my response, anxious now to level with me. 'You guys are clearly fighters, but you've come to the wrong place. You need money for treatment here, and the state hospital can't help you without the correct documentation. Unless it's

146

an emergency, of course.'

'This *is* an emergency!' I snap, boiling over now. I glance at Misha, standing close beside me. 'Does he have to fall down in front of you first?'

A strong hand on my arm now. The guard insisting that I cool it.

'My advice is to go home,' the doctor says. 'You're aliens here. If you're caught up in our system, you could face all kinds of complications. As a minor, your brother might even be taken into care.'

'He's in care already,' I say, shaking with rage now. '*My* care. He just needs treatment. Medicine. Anything to make him better.'

The doctor turns to Misha, if only to stop a scene. He cups his elbow with one hand, props his chin with the other. 'How do you feel?' he asks.

My brother turns to me first, as if seeking my permission to speak. 'Tired,' he says, finally. 'And thirsty.'

The doctor stands tall, nodding now like his mind is made up. 'Give him plenty to drink, find a place to sleep, and then get out of Moscow, for both your sakes.'

'But why?' I say, my voice breaking at the unfairness of it all.

'Because if you stay,' he warns, almost reluctantly, just as the security guard takes over, 'this city will devour you!'

The Dynamo Ice Palace, Leningrad Prospect, Moscow. Near dark:

Tonight, this great stadium stands empty. A ring of light masts loom over the bleachers. On evening fixtures the blaze can be seen for miles. Right now, on the eve of another season, it's just a dark crucible set back among trees. The gates and the kiosks are shuttered, and the last of the autumn leaves lie curled up and frozen in the gutters.

In place of the roar of a crowd, all that can be heard is some random shouting from the parkland behind, and two boys moving briskly through the shadows.

There they go now, stalking the service lane behind the stadium. The frost is thickening here, turning to ice in places. It crackles underfoot like ground glass, and makes the ground quite treacherous. One slip, one misplaced step, and bones could easily be broken.

The taller boy, Alexi, leads the way, clutching the younger one's hand. Misha, his little brother, has a blanket wrapped around his shoulders, but it's way too thin to keep out this bitter cold. Together, they hug the foot of the stadium, testing every hangar door and window, always glancing into the night.

Palettes, empty crates and flattened cardboard boxes are piled up high beside some of the hangars. Carefully, Alexi picks his way up one such stack and pauses at the highest point. There's a fire escape retracted just above him, which he can't quite reach to haul down. He tries jumping, which just causes this haphazard heap to shift and sag. He almost connects on another attempt, but this time a disturbance beneath his feet persuades him to crouch and hiss, 'what was that?'

Misha tightens his blanket in response, only to leap away when the boxes at the base burst apart and a black hound breaks into the night. The smaller boy watches the dog take flight, and then spins back around as the pile slides apart with his brother still at the summit.

Alexi is the first to break the silence that follows the collapse. A giggle, then an outright laugh, before his brother submits just the same. He picks himself up, shushing Misha as best he can, and then laughs again at the opportunity this moment has opened up behind the refuse: a door kicked in at the base, just big enough for a street dog to slip through, or two desperate, disorientated kids in need of a place of safety.

20

I feel like we are inside the belly of a beast. Not just this sports palace we have found, but within the city itself. It started with a warning, that parting shot from a doctor enslaved to procedures, and it has troubled me ever since. In the week that we have been holed out here, I lie awake feeling like we are being slowly broken down and digested.

Seven days we have been inside this hideaway, with each night spent thinking we might never survive to see each sunrise. The space we have unearthed is in the basement, tiled from floor to ceiling, and divided by a long bench. The frost may not reach us in here, and with cardboard sheets for blankets we can just about keep the cold at bay. What gets to me is the damp. A sort of mouldering moisture that puts paid to my attempts to set a fire. Every morning it runs down the only window to bring in any light, despite looking out into a pit capped by bars. On a bright day, the faintest trace of warmth can also draw out a musky, feral stink. Most of the time this place just smells like a changing room in disrepair, though Mish is quick to blame my feet.

His sense of humour is the one thing that keeps me going. For in most other ways my brother has become withdrawn. Not just from me but the world around.

The first night, a few minutes after I had dragged some cardboard sheeting inside, he suffered another seizure. Not a minor one, not a major one, but to call it a 'moment' any longer was just hiding from the truth. This time, it was enough to make me cry. Had I not been so exhausted myself, I would've carried him back to that cursed hospital and hunted down the medic who had turned us away. When Mish came round, he kept touching one temple and wincing. At first, I thought he was in pain. It was only when he began speaking again that I wondered if he had simply been trying to reconnect with his mind. To begin, he had a problem remembering my name – and even his own at times. I had to remind him of most things, apart from why we were here. I kept this last piece of the jigsaw to myself. He didn't question what we were doing in this squalid hole, so I held it back. I decided either he didn't want to be reminded of his condition, or he had simply opened his eyes to his surroundings and assumed it was where we belonged.

Little Mish might seem strangely settled, but I feel trapped. Like a wounded animal, weak and vulnerable to predators, we have gone to ground on instinct. I could take him to a public hospital, but the risk of losing him to the authorities is just unthinkable. I have also considered slipping back over the steppes by railroad, and heading for Almaty with our tails between our legs. I feel guilty for not turning around with Tao, and wish I had seen this city through her eyes. Now she has gone it feels like we travelled here with some kind of ghost. I am haunted by

152

her, in many ways, but like to believe she turned her back on Moscow rather than us. With time on my hands to think and reflect, I realise that we should have done the same thing. The hospitals here might offer everything I could wish for my brother – I just hadn't stopped to consider that the doors would be closed to us. What Tao's absence proves to me, however, is that going home would in no way be an admission of defeat.

Outside our territory, it seems to me, we are good as dead.

Before I can think about stowing away by train again, little Mish needs to regain his strength and spirit. Right now he is unable to make it outside. He depends upon me just as I have depended on him in the past. My crew would never have laid claim to so much precious space junk without him, after all. He has been my eyes for me many times over, on the former seabed and all the way out here. That's why I consider it to be my duty to look out for him until he is ready to leave.

So I keep refilling his water bottle with frost scraped from the parkland grass, and spend my days foraging for food.

I have not travelled far to find scraps. I am too scared to leave Mish alone for long periods. I am also frightened I might get lost. What I have discovered is that in Moscow, dawn is the best time to cross avenues. The traffic is scarce at this hour, and the roadkill uncovered by the rising sun warns me never to make a dash for it in darkness.

Only this morning, having ventured out to the prospect

in front of the stadium. I count three canine bodies across the asphalt. Mostly, it's the way these dogs are lying that suggest something other than sleep, also the frost in their pelts. Those cars and trucks that are out at this hour simply weave around the corpses, just as I do when I sprint for the other side. There are a lot of strays out here. I have seen them roaming in packs, which is something I miss myself. It makes me think of my crew and also the Molotov Horde. We were sworn enemies, but in numbers we always survived. Even if some fell on the way, as one we would never die.

On the other side, behind the hotel further down, I have found a broad alley with access to the kitchens. The bins are almost always full to overflowing, and from there I have collected rye bread for my brother, salted fish and even mutton shanks. The dogs, I quickly realised, are competition. As I round the corner now, my arms folded tight against this early-morning chill, I find bins overturned and refuse sacks that look more like spilled guts. It seems the scavengers before me know how to remove all the good stuff, leaving just slops, drool and that pungent marking scent. There might be one or two titbits in there, but the stink is just too much for me.

Instead, as I discover this morning, it is possible to slip into the kitchen without anyone noticing. I have to watch from behind the bins for a while, and wait for the chef in there to work at the surfaces on the far side. I see him collect a rack of lamb from the delivery store and then set it down beside his knives. When he begins to work on it, I ease my way through the polythene strips that hang

154

from the door. The heat from the ovens is just beautiful, but that isn't why I'm here. I grab a bag of fresh donuts, a tub of what looks like cooked meatballs in gravy, and then brace myself for the outside world again. It might take my breath away, but at least I have fuel for our bellies.

When I return, I find Misha sitting out in the pale sunshine. Judging by his fragile smile on seeing me, it has clearly been a journey in itself for him to get this far. Even so, I think the food I have will soon restore his strength.

'I wanted to see the sky,' is his explanation, when I ask what he is doing.

I settle beside him, squint upwards with one eye. 'I don't suppose you'll spot many rockets going up from here.'

Little Mish is sitting back against the tumbledown pile of cardboard and crates. He's wrapped up against the cold in the blanket still, his legs outstretched, looking like some of the beggars I have seen. The broken door is still fairly well hidden, and I figure we can make a quick exit through it, should anyone appear. Mostly, however, the service lane is our own. Wandering drunks and security patrols seem to have been our only visitors, but none of them hang around for long enough to investigate. I hand my kid brother a donut, and break one apart myself.

'Tastes good,' he says, chewing on my offering. 'We should keep some for Papa.'

I finish my donut in silence, wondering if he is ready

for me to spell out just how far we are from home. 'We can see him again,' I say eventually. 'Just as soon as you think you can make it.'

He says nothing, just helps himself to another donut from the bag.

Keep building up your strength, I say to myself, *and pray that we can get out of here before another moment finds you.*

My brother peers at the sky once again. He looks at it like he's never appreciated such a view before, as if all memory of falling boosters has been wiped entirely from his mind. It is crisp and blue over the city, but cloud thickens to the east. Snow is on the way, it seems, if the sharpening breeze is anything to go by. Like Mish, I am learning to rise above the cold. Even so, it frequently threatens to get the better of me. I keep losing sensation in my fingers and my feet. When that happens, mostly at night and on the streets, I keep telling myself that there is a fire inside me. It is a blaze that has fuelled our journey this far, and which won't be extinguished by the elements.

'Here's something to warm you up,' I say, and peel off the lid covering the meatballs. I pluck out one for my brother, curse it for dripping down my fingers, and find his attention has locked onto something much closer to earth than before.

'Don't move,' he says, quietly.

'Huh?'

I shift my gaze across the service lane, see only a mangy dog slip through the rails from the park. It's really just skin and bone. A dung-coloured mongrel so thin it can push through the bars – and I don't like it one bit. I glance around, ignoring my brother's request now, looking for a stone or stick to shoo it away.

'Let it come,' he says, sounding just a little fractious.

I turn to face him again, surprised by his manner with me. Without a word, he takes the meatball I had been offering him and throws it into the centre of the lane.

'What are you doing?' I ask, amazed.

'Isn't it beautiful?'

'Are you crazy? It looks *diseased*!'

'Shhh!'

The dog is on the concrete now, moving cautiously towards the titbit. It is a feral-looking thing with pale-yellow eyes, a matted pelt and a hungry face. It looks up at us one more time and then throws its jaws over the meatball.

'Misha, you really mustn't encourage something like this. What is it with you and dogs, anyhow . . . Mish!'

Another meatball slaps onto the lane, midway between the mutt and us this time.

'It's starving,' he says brightly. 'Just trying to survive in the city like us.'

'Not on our supplies, it won't!' I am up on my feet before he can protest, clapping my hands to chase it away. The dog skitters sideways from me, keeping low as if expecting me to strike out.

'Leave it alone!' Misha screams so loud that I spin around to shut him up.

'Do you want security to find us here? Keep quiet, brother!'

He struggles to his feet, his vulnerability matched in

that moment by this sudden rage. But what alarms me most of all is the barking at my heels.

The dog had retreated at first, but when I snapped at Mish it came right back again. I spin around, which is enough to persuade the cowardly stray to back off for a beat. Then I return to my brother, my patience stretched now.

'Let him eat with us!' Mish makes this demand without once taking his eyes from me. For a moment we glare at one another. I am first to break it, though, distracted as I am by the dog. The damn thing is switching back and forth behind me again, still making an almighty noise.

'OK!' I give in, and spread my hands. 'But mark my words, you'll be sorry when it won't leave you alone.'

21

The snow began to fall late afternoon. I had been out searching for food much of the day: hunting down fresh restaurant kitchens and then begging in vain from the cooks when I found nothing fit to eat. Just before the weather turned, I had found myself drawn towards a spectacular cathedral. Many buildings shape the skyline here, both faceless and magnificent, but this one was just breathtaking – painted in bright circus colours, and finished with swirling domes, towers and spires. More importantly to me, I discovered other street kids in the big square behind it. All of them were busy hassling passing pedestrians for money. None gave up as their targets hurried across this huge expanse. I admired their persistence, as if each one was a challenge they had to see to the bitter end. The colour of the cobbles made me think of old blood, but all that changed when the first flakes started coming down, soft and light as feathers.

The kids in the square seemed to know each other. After a short while, it became clear they were suspicious of me. I didn't like their hostile looks, but I had to make a little money. Just enough for some bread, perhaps. With the snow settling, I had headed down the hill towards a bridge across the river, and kept walking until I found the entrance to a Metro station. At the foot of the stairs, loitering beside the ticket booth until dusk, I made a total of twelve roubles. The money bought me a loaf, as well as a certain confidence.

I am not born to thrive in this city, as I have discovered, but I can survive. It is really a question of following my instinct, just like I did by targeting the Metro: a warm place below street level where people heading home from work had loose change to hand.

And now, on hurrying back to the basement behind the stadium, I discover that my brother has also found a way to take care of himself. My first thought, in fact, is that he is thriving against all odds. For there he is, asleep in the corner on a pile of flattened boxes. With not one dog curled up beside him, but two. My appearance in this gloomy space prompts one to prick up its ears. I recognise its pale-yellow eyes next, but all it does is watch me as I shake the snow from my shoulders and take to another corner. There, I gnaw on my share of the bread in silence. I don't offer any to the dog, but nor does it hassle me. I suspect it knows where the next scraps will be coming from, and worry that little Mish has been going without. With the last light fading from the space, I scratch at my scalp and settle down as best I can. I find it hard to get comfortable. My bones ache on the cold tiles, and I rearrange myself several times over. When I finally close my eyes, my last thought is that my back is turned from my brother.

* * *

160

The dogs are gone next morning. I even wonder if I had dreamed of their presence. I awake to find Mish at the window. A pelt of snow has settled in the little pit below the bars, while the sky above it is a brilliant white.

'Just look.' My brother turns to face me. I am shocked by the shadows under his eyes. For a boy who has slept so deeply, he looks exhausted. That he's so lively is unsettling. I am surprised he has the energy, and wonder what is driving him now. 'It's so pure,' he adds, though I haven't even glanced through the bars. 'It feels like a fresh start, Alexi.'

Outside, despite the chill, it does indeed seem as if the city has been cleansed. Snow blankets every tree, rooftop and spire, and it's still falling fast. Misha may seem pale and drawn to me, but at least his sense of wonder has returned. I blow on my hands to warm them, unable to rub my palms together on account of the scabs, and wish this could be the day we left. Beyond the railings, the parkland looks unspoiled under this fall. I want us to be first to score our footprints through the drifts. I simply need to know that Mish is up to the long journey that awaits us beyond this sparkling scene. Having half killed him getting here, I will not leave until I am certain that he is ready to go himself. I want to be sure of something else before I head out into the streets in search of something we can eat. Before I mention it, however, I tell him that I love him.

'I know,' he says, bewildered all the same.

'Then promise you won't waste your food by feeding the dogs. You need to get strong, little brother, but I can't be here for you night and day. You have to help yourself here.'

He looks up at me and blinks. 'It isn't a waste,' he says to correct me.

I raise a finger to argue my point, but find I have nothing to say. He looks up at me with wide, unblinking eyes, as if amazed that I would have a problem with his new companions.

'How is your head?' I ask, if only to break the silence.

He keeps a bead on me a moment longer, then dips down to scoop some snow. He packs it into one palm. Glancing my way, he grins and then throws it as hard as he can. The snowball travels surprisingly far, right over the railings and into the trees. We hear it break apart, but it's too far gone to see. 'Beat that,' he says, defiantly.

The next night, shivering against the wall once more, and with my scalp itching madly, I begin to realise that there is more to his generosity with the food than I had first thought. The temperature has plumbed new depths, turning the snow to stone, it seems, even freezing the damp that has seeped into my clothes. I cannot fight the cold much longer. It keeps dragging me from sleep, but not little Mish. Two more dogs have joined his cardboard lair, I see. These ones are bigger than the mongrel and his mate, while the smell is intense. I want to get up to clear them away. I also want to join them, curled together in a heap, but I am just too worn out by it all. Even so, as I ball up as best I can, I tell myself that it can't go on. These dogs have come from the streets. This is their world, not ours, and they could turn on us at any time. I will speak to him, I decide. For whatever reason he has stopped listening to me, I will find some way to get through.

Except, the next morning, when I pick myself up from the floor, I discover little Mish has gone. He isn't by the window, and nor is he outside. The dogs have disappeared, so too has my brother, and I am seized by dread and panic.

'Misha!' I keep to the pavements that have been cleared. The snow here is piled up at the sides. It is stained like a fresh bruise and smells of the chemical treatment used to melt it away. Everywhere the brilliant whiteness is beginning to discolour, but only one thing concerns me. 'Misha! *Where the hell are you?*'

I cover both sides of the big avenue, thankful only that this snowfall has slowed the traffic so I stand at least a chance of skating across safely. I even cover the alley behind the kitchen. I know Mish has never been there, but I once told him of the food I had found in it. Even so, he is nowhere to be seen. Just freshly upturned bins and paw prints in the drifts. I try hard to stay calm. I keep telling myself that he has a nose for survival just as I have. He is tough. A son of Aral. I cling to this conviction as I seek out the hospital, retracing every step he might have taken. Despite everything, I can't help thinking Moscow must seem so vast for a small boy like him. Even I feel dwarfed here. As I scour the avenue, passing the spot on the opposite side where we first arrived in this city, I wonder whether Tao had foreseen that we would be slowly frozen out. By the time I come through the crash doors of the hospital, the warm air inside actually hurts my lungs.

'You again? From the other week?'

The guard rushes up to block my path. Panting violently, with my hands on my knees, I look at him and shake my head.

'I've lost my brother,' I say through chattering teeth. 'Is he here?'

'Like the man spelled out last time, there is nothing for you at this address.'

I focus on his face, trying hard to stop shivering and stay on my feet. 'You have to help,' I plead, but the guard has had enough. He spins me round. I feel his palm in the small of my back, see the doors opening. They swing apart, but in towards me not out into the snow, and there is the man himself. Same white coat and stethoscope, but with a look of shock and surprise when his eyes rise to mine.

'My God.' He turns to the guard, then back to me with some concern. 'And where is the little boy?'

Just hearing him say this helps me to get a grip. I tell him he is missing, in a stammering whisper first and then with some force. The doctor glances at the guard once more and across to the reception staff. A telephone rings. When the nurse picks up finally, she has to clear her throat before speaking.

'I can't let street kids inside,' the guard says under his breath, as if reminding him of something he has been told many times before. 'Respect my position, Doctor. If the Director shows up we'll both be fired.'

The doctor finds my gaze again. He reaches for the back of his head, embarrassed but strangely amused by something. I just look him square in the eyes, hoping and praying that he won't turn away from me again.

'Do you smoke?' he asks next, which makes me laugh despite myself.

'Sure,' I say. 'Though it has been a while since I tasted a cigarette.'

He draws a crumpled soft-top pack from his inside pocket, says: 'We'll have to step outside to light up. Hospital rules. We should go now before you warm up too fast. Can you handle that?'

'Let's do it.' I shrug the guard's paw from my shoulder, bracing myself for the cold again, and lead the way through the doors.

22

'Smoking kills,' I say, and draw deeply on my cigarette. The ember brightens defiantly. I cup the tip in my palm, the filter pinched between my thumb and finger, and watch it quiver there. I am so very cold and worried for my brother, but somehow this feels like a break from the worst of it. 'Where I come from,' I continue, 'smoking is the least of our worries. But what's a man of medicine doing with a deadly habit like this?'

The doctor examines his own tube, leaning into the rail like me. We've lit up on the raised entrance in front of the hospital. An ambulance has just pulled in under the canopy behind us. The engine is still running, thickening the air with exhaust fumes.

'Wherever you are in the world,' he says, 'there are plenty of things that can kill you first.'

'Like cars,' I say, scratching at my head again. 'In a city like yours.'

He smiles, taps ash into the snow below us. 'Like cars.'

'It's what I'll remember about this place, when we leave.'

'The traffic can be fierce at times,' he agrees. 'But I don't believe that stopped you making it to the station.'

I tell him that we had holed up so my brother could rest, just like he had advised us. Only he got sick again, I explain, and frankly I hadn't known what I should do for the best. This time, unlike our first encounter, he listens to every word I have to say. I tell him our names, our ages, and how we had found out way out here. He draws long on his cigarette, and lets me share everything Mish and I have been through. 'All I want to do now is take him back to our country,' I stress. 'I was just waiting until he found his strength again.'

'And now he's vanished?' the doctor asks, checking he has understood me. 'At least he's back on his feet.'

I feel my chest tighten, struggle to hold back tears. 'It's so unlike him to disappear without me. But he's changed since we've been here.'

'If he's experienced seizures as you say, it may well have had an impact on his character. People have been known to surface with no knowledge of their own identity, or even see life in new ways. Sometimes it can appear like they're functioning on an entirely different level, especially in the way they interact with others. The brain is a mystery to us, Alexi, but also very tough. It can suffer all kind of trauma and come through with the basic instincts intact.'

'You make him sound like a primitive.'

'Or a warrior.' He shrugs, flick the stub of his cigarette into the snow below. 'It's clearly in the blood.'

'I just want him back.' I wipe my cheeks with the heel of one hand. 'Even if I can't make Misha right again, at least I should be with him. I've even started losing him to a pack of damn dogs. They keep him warm at night, in return for food.'

'He has your instinct for survival, Alexi. You should be relieved.'

'Part of me feels like he's shutting me out, though. It's as if things have got so bad for us he's chosen his own way to get through.'

'You'll always be there for each other,' says the doctor, facing me now. 'Misha will know that, in his heart, no matter what's going on inside his mind. I also think you shouldn't give up on him.'

'I'll never do that,' I say defiantly.

'Then go back to the one place here that he knows. Wherever it is you've been hiding out, it's probably the centre of his world right now.' He pauses there, thinking to himself. Then, with a sigh, he reaches for his pocket, produces a wallet and slips out several notes. 'And when you track him down, Alexi, use this money to go back where *you* know. It isn't much, but should be enough to bribe your way across the border, if necessary. Whatever kind of medical care is available over there, at least you have some rights to it. Here, my friend, you don't exist. You and your brother are nothing. You might as well be ghosts.' He hands me the money. I can't feel the paper between my frozen fingers, but I see it clearly. 'Just be sure to go home this time, Alexi. This is no place for boys like you. You're dangerously cold, half starved and lice-ridden.' He picks at my hair, finds something there, and flicks it away in disgust. Now you really must leave before I lose my job.'

I can't find the right words, if only because I am choked. I look up at him and offer my hand. In response he shows me his palms, muttering something about transmission risks, and turns for the crash doors.

I cut through the parkland on my way back to the stadium. It is quicker this way, and I realise that since my arrival in Moscow I have at last begun to get my bearings. The snow here remains largely untouched. It weighs heavily in the poplar trees. The skies are clearing, too. The cloud cover has broken up in places, and sunshine pushes through. For once, I even feel some warmth on my face. Flakes are still falling, but the worst is over, I think to myself. In this light, and after such an act of human kindness, the city doesn't feel so bad. It may not be for me, I realise now I'm here, but at least I have the determination and at last the means to get away.

All I need now is my brother.

With every step I remind myself of the doctor's advice. That Misha will return to what he knows. I keep to the path, crunching through grit, and avoid the glances and glares from the people here: old soldiers on benches, mothers with small children wrapped up against the freeze, and all the lost souls like me. I can spot those who live on the streets with ease now. Whatever their age, very few are dressed in rags. Some seem quite smart, in fact. A few of the elderly types sport suits that simply need a good wash. But what all of them share is a certain rawness. I imagine they can see the same thing in me, if only I were to meet their gaze.

When I do look up, it is simply to check I am heading in the right direction. I can see the stadium through the poplars, and follow the path that steers towards it. A couple of businessmen trudge towards me, wearing greatcoats, scarves and stately fur hats. I move aside to let them pass, avoid their eyes as I do so, and glimpse movement to my right. There it is again, way off the path in a distant glade. Not deer, I think at first, but dogs running in a pack. They're almost swarming, it seems to me, loping between the tree trunks in the same direction. One dog breaks off and circles back expectantly. It's big, unnaturally so: a shadow-black mastiff with a sandstone muzzle. What I see next is an upright figure catch up with the hound, before they race together to join the pack. A small boy, I am sure, wrapped in a blanket that billows like a cape.

'*What has become of you?*' I whisper to myself, and tear across the snow in pursuit. '*In God's name, what has happened?*'

I track the paw prints to the railings between the parkland and the avenue. They literally melt away through the bars into slush where the pavement has been treated, but I don't hesitate in heading for the ice palace and the service lane behind it. Sure enough, as I come in sight of the tumbledown boxes, I spot the black mastiff sniffing through the litter at the base. It turns on my approach. Then another emerges from the doorway, coming alert when they see me. I slow to a trot, a different kind of cold clawing into me now, and struggle to appear calm. Both dogs are waist-high and without collars. Turned loose on

171

the streets, I think to myself, when they grew too hard to handle. They watch me approach with interest: heads cocked, front feet planted firmly, braced for my next move.

'Easy now,' I say, circling wide around them for the door. 'I'm here for my brother.'

The dogs keep a steady bead on me. Then one drops down as if preparing to pounce. Drool spills from its slack lips. I keep on moving, as carefully as I can, my sights locked onto the passage we had uncovered. A deep-throated growl starts up, and I tell myself that it's too late now to make a sudden break. My stomach tightens. Knotting with fear and adrenalin. I sense one dog shadow me as I bow into the passage, leaving the daylight behind.

23

'Misha! I've been so worried. What is this?'

My kid brother is standing on the bench inside the old changing room. He's dropped the blanket now, in defiance of the cold. At his feet I count at least a dozen dogs, all different breeds, but similar in size and dark, earthy colours. The rangy mutt who first found us is also among their number. It is smaller than the others, but very much at the heart of the pack. The pair that had met me at the door now slip around to join the others. All of them pace and sway below my brother. Their hot and steamy breath fouls the space, but none appear to have picked up on my presence. In his hands, Misha is holding what looks like a broiled chicken. 'It's feeding time,' he calls across cheerfully. 'Are you hungry?' At this, he rips out a wing at the socket and tosses it into the jaws of the first dog to spring up on its hindquarters. 'I stole this from the kitchen you told me about. There's enough for everyone.'

I am disturbed by what I have found here, and somehow heartened to find him so alert. His clothes and nails and hair may be filthy, and his eyes even deeper set than before, but his spirit is just as the doctor had predicted. If

I have been awaiting a sign that little Mish is ready for the journey, I think to myself, this must be it.

'It's time to go,' I tell him, aware of the money in the pocket of my jeans. 'Wrap the chicken in the blanket for later and let's get out of here.'

'To where?' He looks at me, mystified, and shreds some more white meat for the dogs.

'Home, little brother. We're going home.'

'This is home.'

I have to stand back by a step just to take in what he has said. It might have confirmed what I suspected, but just hearing it feels like a betrayal of our roots. Our grandfather may have hailed from this country, but I know where we belong now. I don't want to be in this place any more. I just assumed he would follow me without question.

'Mish,' I say, as calmly as I can, 'I have money to get us back again. We'll get your treatment from there.'

'There's nothing wrong with me.' He speaks without looking up, still picking away at the goddamn bird. 'I've never felt more alive in my life.'

'Mish! This is me, *Alexi*. I'm telling you it's time to go!'

My outburst is met by silence. Then a single, menacing rumble. It's a growl that could be coming from any of the dogs, the way they all zone in on me. Another one joins in, sounding even more aggressive. Then the barking breaks out.

I stand my ground for a beat, switching my disbelief from the dogs to my kid brother up on the bench. The din is intense and very frightening in this closed space. Slowly, unwillingly, I retreat to the door.

'They won't harm you,' Mish assures me, and takes a greedy bite from the chicken. 'Unless you're a threat.' I watch him chewing casually, unconcerned by the fact that the dogs appear to be held in check by his word only. 'Will you have some?' he shouts across, wiping grease from his chin with the back of his hand. 'You need to eat, Alexi. Really, you should try it. I have never tasted anything so good.'

'Mish, *please . . .*'

'Boy, this city has a lot to offer,' he declares, deaf to my appeal. 'Here!' Without warning, he lobs it across to me. Clumsily, I catch the slimy lump, but it's too much for some of the dogs. One lunges for my prize. I see teeth sink in and then attempt to shake it violently from my hands. I let go immediately but the rest of the pack want a piece now. I see them come around me, the fat on my palms, wrists and chest encouraging them to climb. I feel myself being dragged to the ground by two weighty paws on my back. Black gums and flint-shaped teeth flash in front of my face. I'm sinking still, and push with all my might to regain my footing.

'Call them off!' I yell. 'Do something!'

I cry out for help again, but can't compete with the furious barking. If anything, my plea just escalates the situation. Twisting around now, I try to wade free – only to get a testing nip in the arm for my efforts, followed by a hot pain in my other hand. I scream, but the dog with its fangs in my flesh does not let go.

'Hey!' I hear Mish yell. He sounds afraid now, which gives me just a thread of hope. 'Leave my brother alone!'

I collapse onto my knees, keeping one of the mastiffs away with my free hand. I feel another clamping pain, to my shoulder blade this time. With a roar, I crack my elbow into a canine jaw. I hear a yelp, feel some release, and cry for help one more time. The air in here is thinning, it seems, but I am desperate not to go down, and cling to that thought when I see my brother leaping from the bench. Little Mish wades through flank and tail. A look of pure horror on his face. I wrench my hand free at last, slick with blood and saliva, and shield myself as best I can. All the time I hear him order the dogs to stand away, but they're beyond his control now and he knows it. I shrink from another assault, find a small hand reaching out to me. I push forward, desperate to save myself now, only to see that lifeline drop away.

'Let's go.' I hear my brother's voice over the din, but this time with no trace of fear in it, nor panic or desperation.

I meet his eyes just then, and cry out at the transformation. For despite this storm engulfing us, the horror has left him. Instead, in the moment before those orbs tilt upwards, I see just an absolute calm.

'*No!*' I wail, as he tips back among his pack. 'No more moments, Mish!' Seeing him collapse to the ground just serves to summon the last of my strength. I rise up as he falls, and power towards him. At the same time, the dogs clear away from me and quickly regroup. I am faced, all of sudden, not with an attacking ring but a line of defence.

I try to step around, but they have my brother covered now. The barking, baying and snarling hits new heights, but all I can hear is the wretched noise from behind: the grunts and gasping breath, the dance of limbs on tiles. It is a seizure like no other. The sound of my whole world collapsing.

'Misha!' I hear myself yelling. 'I am here, little brother! Hold on!' I look around, spot a stick amid the rubbish on the floor. Brought here, I figure, by a playful dog. Only now it is a weapon that I grab to arm myself. With all my might, I swing it at the pack. They stand their ground and just rage at me all the more. I try again, from another direction. This time, I connect with a flank. The dog yowls and shrinks from the stick, just long enough for me to glimpse my brother on the floor. His back is arched as if it might snap and vomit is spluttering from his mouth. It's clear to me that he is choking, still shuddering from top to toe. A dog springs between us, furious with me, and more so when I scream right back at it. I use the stick to smack and jab. Blood and mucus fly. I am pushed back by a step, but rally as best I can. And yet the harder I fight, the more I am forced away from my brother. I sense the fire in me begin to flicker, the swipes I make slowly weaken. This pack appears to feed upon my failure, and vainly I try one more time. Weeping with frustration, I wheel the stick in front of me. By now, the dogs are wise to the move. They dip away before I can connect with any of them, but it is enough for me to see that the damage has been done.

For my brother has stopped moving.

There he is, sprawled unnaturally, like a discorded doll. His eyes are back and locked on me, but without any reach or focus. No sign of life in them.

24

I am the first to howl. I drop my stick, throw back my head and let my lungs fill this space. I am breathless when I turn my back on the dogs. They do not attack, but continue their guard as I turn to get away. My eyes smart as I scramble from the passage, but not just by this sudden return of the winter light. *I have to get help*, is all I can think. It blinkers me as I race from the ice palace, heading for the only place I know in this city where someone at least recognises that we exist.

I must find help. My brother needs me.

I splash through slush piles, weaving round pedestrians and setting off dogs that are at least on leashes. The cold air stings my face, but I cannot stop. I know exactly where I'm heading, and I focus on that moment to escape the horror of what I've left behind. I run for what seems like a lifetime, my composure coming undone with every footfall. By the time I reach the hospital, I am stumbling and distraught, and then overcome entirely. Perhaps it is the grit underfoot, there in front of the entrance canopy, or maybe my legs refused to carry me further. Either way, I throw out my hands as I sprawl, and though I try to get up I just can't do it.

For I know it is over now. With nothing here for me, I realise I have simply fled from the truth.

'That's far enough!' A hand grabs me roughly by the scruff. It's the security guard, I see, as he hauls me onto my feet. I watch my hands lift away from the slush, as if my mind has been cut out of my body. 'You just don't give up, do you?'

I try to tell him that it's all too late, but can't find the words between breaths.

He looks me in the eyes, for a beat practically holding me upright. 'If it wasn't for my job . . .' he says, sounding calmer now, and trails off there, like nothing more needs to be said. I nod, filling with tears, and listen to him speak into his radio.

The doctor is outside within minutes. When he sees me, he stops buttoning up his coat and quickens his pace. Together with the guard, he walks me to the wall under the entrance. A lot more ash lies on the snow there, I notice, as he asks the guard to leave us now and sets about examining my wounds.

'Who did this?' he wants to know. 'How did it happen?'

I don't respond. Not until he tips my chin so I am looking directly at him, and asks after my brother. 'Did you find him?'

I nod, and then confess I just lost him again. 'Misha isn't coming back this time,' I add, my eyes filling up once again.

'Where is he?' the doctor demands, grimly concerned.

'*Gone!*' It's all I can tell him, cross with myself for not being in control. I wish I hadn't come. Now that I am here, all I want to do is head right back again, and take care of everything. I wipe my eyes, clear my throat. 'He's gone from here.'

He looks at me searchingly, awaiting more detail. I turn away, but even then I sense him reading me. Indeed, I know exactly what he is going to ask next. I am just not prepared to hear the words.

'Is he dead?'

I close my eyes, squeezing them tight and swallowing hard. He asks me again, and this time I nod if only so he won't repeat the question. Before he can say any more, I find the money in my pocket.

'You've been so kind, but there's no need for this any more.' I stop there and offer him the notes. 'I may not be able to take care of my brother, but I can look after myself from here.'

'Alexi, forget the money. This is serious. Where is he now?'

'It doesn't matter,' I say, and this time I take his hand and press the money into it. 'I should go. I'm sorry I troubled you again.'

'Wait!' He sounds insistent, and blocks my path to the street. 'This is crazy. You need to rest. At the very least let me treat these wounds.'

'I'll heal,' I say, drying my eyes. 'Even if there's scarring.'

'Alexi, I must insist—'

'I said it's *over*!' I feel myself bristling, but not with aggression. I just want him to know this thing is finished.

At first I see some protest in him, but he's read me once already and I want him to read me again.

Finally, the doctor breaks from my glare and turns his attention to the money. The notes look useless in his palm, half-sprung like a crushed cockroach. With a sigh, he closes his fingers around it. 'Alexi, I won't insult you by making you take it, but there is one thing I must insist upon.'

'What is that?'

In response, he unbuttons his jacket, shakes it from his shoulders and hands it to me. 'It's set to get colder still,' he says, pulling up the collar on his white coat underneath. 'I don't care how tough you are, you need warmth.'

The jacket is lined with a fur trim. I become aware of the doctor's body heat just as soon I climb inside it. For a brief moment, I feel safe. He buttons me up, rolls my sleeves to fit.

'Thank you,' I whisper, and offer to shake his hand. It's only when he fails to take it that I remember his reluctance the last time. 'I'm sorry,' I say, and hide my palm, not knowing what to think now.

'So am I,' he says. I look up into his face again; his eyes start to turn wet. 'I'm really very sorry this had to happen,' he adds, and spreads his arms uselessly.

And there in his embrace, everything I have tried to hold back heaves out in great sobs.

When I drift back to the ice palace, I am wrapped up against the freeze. Even so, I feel entirely numb. I hear

182

the dogs howling before I reach the service road. This time, I don't want to join in. I choose to stay outside, slumped beside the passage with my head in my hands. I listen to the pack mark the passing of their companion, barely able to believe it myself. Their keening will continue for some hours, until the distant sun begins to sink behind the trees. The cold lays claim to my extremities, but it really does come as a comfort. The less I feel right now the better, both inside and out. I sense an unspeakable sadness hanging over me. I just can't let it fall yet. Not until I have done my duty as a brother.

The pack file out at dusk. Some brush me as they pass, but I don't flinch or strike out at them. When the final dog leaves, the wolfish-one with the pale eyes, I creep back inside and begin my own wake. I may stay here one more night, in a decaying basement under an ice palace, in a city as cruel and unforgiving as an old seabed, but a world away from what I know.

Kneeling on the floor, I haul my brother's body into my arms. I close his eyelids with my thumbs. When I find my voice, I talk to him at length about the life we shared together and all the things that might have been. Throughout, I stroke his hair and face – licked clean by the grieving pack. I tell him that if heaven is as wild as it is here on earth, then I have every faith that he will find his place in no time.

Once I say my final goodbye at dawn, emerging into the light to find a subdued, waiting pack, I will set my sights on returning to Aral. I face great peril there, maybe even the same sickness as my brother, but it is where I belong. I will leave the parkland for the railway lines, aiming to follow in Tao's footsteps. This strange angel may have come into our lives just briefly, but she had shown me a way out. Should anyone stare at me in shock or disgust, I pledge to stare them down this time. I may be battle-scarred and frozen to the bone, but one emotion is sure to thaw, and that is a strange kind of pride.

Pride for my brother, shot through with love.

The dogs will take care of him. This, I accept when they return for their soul mate. What I take away is one small comfort that can only strengthen and endure: a belief, at last, that someone is watching over me. I may be fragile and exhausted, but I will never be alone. I hope it will give me the determination to grow stronger, so I may be ready again to assemble my crew. For even if The Bat brings a war to my door once more, it would be nothing compared to this. I am prepared for my father, too. He will recognise that I put everything into this stand, and we can grieve together. As a comfort, I shall assure him that his youngest son found just what he was looking for. And should we ever need to be reminded of him, we shall simply lift our gaze to the satellites and stars above. Finally, my thoughts must turn to Lena, and her promise to keep a place for me in her heart. I may have avenues and borders to cross, but whatever I face when I get there, I will find my way home.